Just another case of

When a WWII supe. can transform back into a man by being intimate with a woman, he seeks to free the rest of his unit via some unconventional matchmaking.

But how do you find a woman willing to take a chance on a spoon?

Cheryl isn't prepared to hear her friend is getting it on with a Fork.

Or that her friend's hot fiancé is the result.

Cheryl wants nothing to do with their cutlery kink . . . until she holds the spoon for the first time and it feels meant to be.

The dating pool has proven unsatisfying.

Battery-operated devices don't cuddle you afterward.

Your friend claims a kind-hearted, huge, super soldier is trapped in your spoon, and only you can free him.

Wouldn't you give it a try?

Just once?

Just to make sure?

SPOONED

A Lighthearted Utensil Romance
Book 2

Ruth Cardello

Author Contact
website: RuthCardello.com
email: rcardello@ruthcardello.com
Facebook: Author Ruth Cardello
TikTok: tiktok.com/@author.ruthcardello

Copyright

This book is dedicated to:

Anyone who has ever tried to please someone else so much that they lost themselves along the way. You were always enough. Be you and be proud.

Trigger warning:
This novella is about a World War II super soldier, trapped inside a spoon, who can only take human form by being intimate with a woman. The author attempted to keep the spooning jokes to a minimum, but some may have slipped through.

Note to my readers

Why did *Spooned* take months to come out, when it's a novella? The answer lies in a promise I made my husband way back in 2012 . . .

Back when we couldn't pay our electricity and our cable bill in the same month.

Back when our youngest was a toddler and our oldest was in high school and even though we worked full-time jobs, we still cleaned the home of a family member for extra money because children are expensive.

Back when we thought that maybe, just maybe, my writing might bring in a sustainable second income.

My husband and I sat down and imagined our lives if my career took off. We dreamed of paying off our debt and all the places we'd travel together.

But we also wanted to keep each other grounded, so we talked about what we'd have to do to get to a better financial place and what our definition of success should be.

We made this list of our priorities, so that no matter where this writing career took us, we wouldn't lose focus on what's important.

Our list also became a promise to each other:

We want to stay happily married.

We want to be present in the lives of our children and family.

We want to be healthy both mentally and physically.

For over a decade, that list has guided our decisions with my career as well as his. Nothing is ever perfect, and it's impossible to excel in all areas of your life at all times, but whenever the constant juggling feels like too much, or we start to doubt ourselves, we return to that list, and it centers us. Twelve years in the publishing industry, and we're still happily married and best friends. Our children keep us busy, but that's the blessing of having them.

Lately my books are taking a little longer to come out because I'm focusing on my family. Our youngest is in high school now and time flies by too quickly. In a heartbeat this stage of our lives will end and my writing time will be less frequently interrupted. I both look forward to and dread that day.

Time goes so quickly.

I'm also a grandmother now. *A grandmother.* What a wonderful reminder that life is beautiful in all its stages.

I'm physically fluffier than I wish I were, but I'm active and every day I resolve to do better. It's a battle. Those who have spent a lifetime struggling with their weight will understand.

I get most of my mental health from my horses, but that's another story . . .

I wrote **Forked** during a tough time when I needed to work on something silly. Now, I have laughed my way through writing **Spooned** and can't wait to share it with you. **Knifed** is next.

If these books don't completely tank my writing career, people have suggested that I continue the series. Some want a set of three utensils with one heroine in a utensil why choose. I'd love to write a spin-off novella about the child of one of the utensils . . . and the title will be . . . **Sporked**. The possibilities are endless and so much fun to imagine.

It's my hope that my venture into the genre of utensil romances brings others the same kind of escapism amusement as it brought me.

Careful, though, I can no longer look at large, decorative wall utensils with a straight face. I also giggle every time someone says they have a favorite utensil.

When you know, you know.

Chapter One

Cheryl

Providence, Rhode Island
2024

"WOULD YOU LIKE a beer?" I ask as I slip off my shoes and head to my kitchen, waving for my friend Greg to follow. "I need one after today."

Greg slides onto one of the leather barstools at the granite island that sold me on the downtown Providence apartment. The expansive surface is stunning and multi-functional. Not only can I gather my friends around it for a board-game marathon, but I can also lay out several maps side by side or sort through folders of not yet digitized documents on whatever topic I'm currently researching for amusement.

"Sure. Did one of your clients forget to tell you you're brilliant?" he asks lightly. "You had to break it to them that you only helped them make millions instead of billions?"

For an intelligent man, Greg can act an idiot well. I roll my eyes. "We can't all save the world like you do."

His grin is a little smug. We're both research analysts who enjoy reading scientific studies for fun, but that's where our similarities end. Greg comes from a family of blue-collar workers. His parents are proud of him simply for graduating from college and finding employment. I'm not sure they even know what he does for the Water Pollution Control Commission.

I do, because he tells me all the time the reason he loves his job is because he feels like he's making a difference. His recommendations are often what the lobbyists use to shape new regulations and laws.

My parents were disappointed when I chose to not continue school after receiving my master's degree. I love to learn new things, but I don't enjoy being told how or what. My decision to work as a freelance market analyst allows me to make a comfortable income while still having a life outside of work and the freedom to focus on anything I'm interested in.

Someone with my IQ could have skipped high school and should be working on their second PhD.

Am I aware that intelligence without sustained effort and dedication results in mediocrity?

Oh, I'm aware. I've only heard that speech every summer since I chose softball over science camp.

Yes, I was offered the opportunity to test out of high

school early, but I didn't want to. I wanted to play sports, have friends, date, and go to prom.

I don't consider life a race in which I've fallen behind. Life isn't measured only by achievements. Isn't it also about living? Laughing? Finding someone to share our limited trips around the sun with?

I retrieve two bottles of beer, open them, then place one in front of Greg before gulping down half of mine. He watches me, not touching his. "Sorry," he says. "What's going on?"

I sigh. Should I tell him? It might have been an elaborate joke. Maybe I missed the punchline. "Mercedes asked me to drop by her place earlier today."

"And?" Greg tips his head to one side, and his mop of hair bounces across his forehead. Tall and lean, he's undeniably attractive, but sadly, for whatever reason, he's not my type. I've given myself a few stern talks in the mirror about why he should be, but when he looks at me—I feel nothing more than friendship.

My next gulp of beer neither calms my nerves nor lessens my confusion. "Have you met Hugh?"

"Her live-in boyfriend? Yes. He's a little odd, but I like him."

"What do you know about him?"

"Not a lot. Just that he left for a while but is back and they seem happy together." His head tips again in the other direction, reminding me of a golden retriever trying to figure out what a person is saying. "Why?"

I don't like to say anything negative about people in my social circle and, through Greg, Mercedes has joined our small group of friends. "I like Mercedes . . ."

"But?"

"I'm concerned that she may not be . . ."

"Be what?"

"Psychologically stable. She seemed fine when you brought her over for games on research nights, but some of what she said to me today made me think Hugh might be affecting her mental well-being."

"Wow, that's a strong statement."

Yeah. I don't like that I said it aloud. As someone who knows the sting of constantly being evaluated and found wanting, I try never to judge anyone. Today was weird, though, and I need to talk it out with someone. "It's possible I misunderstood them. The conversation was jumbled."

Greg nods. "What did they say?"

Swirling the contents of the bottle, I stall as I choose my next words. I promised Mercedes and Hugh that I wouldn't share their secret, but does such a promise count if they're clinically delusional? I decide to start with what they said about me. "I'm single."

Greg's eyebrows knit together. "I know."

"And it's been a while since I've . . . ah . . . met anyone I was interested in."

"I'm listening." His eyes widen. We get together once a

week with our other friends to hang out, but we don't share too much of our personal lives. I don't know why.

I wave my hands in front of me. "I'm twenty-six and spend a lot of time alone, but I'm happy. Even if someone magically appeared, I'm not looking for a relationship." I make a face. "And I don't believe in magic."

Greg blinks a few times quickly. "There's nothing wrong with being single or alone. It's called being selective with your time."

He doesn't understand. How could he? I have a spoon in my purse that Mercedes and Hugh tried to convince me harbors a World War II super soldier.

It's in my purse.

And I can't stop thinking about it.

I don't know why I took it. Mercedes started telling me some wild story about having sex with a fork and how that had brought them together and I couldn't get out of there fast enough. I don't care what the two of them do in the privacy of their bedroom or if it involves cutlery, but I should have told them I wasn't interested in joining their kink club.

Instead of calmly handing the spoon back to Mercedes, I bolted with it. Now, here I am, wondering who is more mentally troubled—them for their little utensil obsession or me for letting this become a bigger issue than it should be.

Since Greg's the one who introduced Mercedes to our circle of friends, I could ask him to return it to her. I could lie and say I borrowed it by accident. He doesn't need to know the details surrounding it.

I'm not a good liar.

And I can't tell him the truth.

Mercedes and Hugh aren't endangering anyone. There must be a simple, non-confrontational way to handle this. "Greg, can I ask you something . . . something personal?"

He leans forward. "Anything."

"If you had a secret kink and you shared it with someone and they weren't into it, how would you want them to tell you?"

Interest sparks in his eyes. "Is there something you want to say, Cheryl?"

I nod with relief. "There is. But I can't. I shouldn't. I'm not going to. I just want to make sure—"

He lays a hand over mine. "Cheryl, I'm open-minded. I'll admit that until today I thought all you wanted was friendship, but you and I get along well. We could fuck and see how it goes."

"Oh." *No. No. No.* I pull my hand away. "I'm sorry. You think I'm . . . ah . . . because I said kink . . ." I swallow hard.

He sits back with a grin. "This is awkward, isn't it? It doesn't have to be. We're both adults and, like you said, single. I don't know what you're into, but I'm willing to try most things once."

I clumsily rise to my feet. Inviting Greg over to talk had been a mistake. "That's good to know, Greg. I'll keep that in mind. For now, I think you should . . ."

He comes to stand over me and kisses me gently. I want it to be a sensational kiss, one that wipes the earlier nonsense out of my head, but it isn't, and it doesn't. It's sweet, but when he breaks it off, it doesn't leave me wanting a second. I shake my head and step back. "Well, okay, you should go."

The concern in his expression seems sincere. "We don't have to fuck if you don't want to."

I hug my arms around myself. "I don't want to."

He frowns and looks around. "I must have misread the situation. You've never invited me here alone. Then the beer. And the way you were talking . . . I thought . . ."

I walk to the door of my apartment and hold it open. "I know. I'm an idiot. Could we pretend this didn't happen?"

"Sure. I guess." He scratches the back of his neck.

"Awesome." I tap my foot nervously. "Thanks for coming by."

"I just got here."

"Yeah." I wave a hand toward the door. "But . . ."

He frowns. "Why are you acting so weird?"

I open the door. "I handled this wrong. Don't feel bad."

"I didn't do anything to feel bad about. Unless you're upset that I kissed you."

For just a moment I hide my eyes behind one hand, then face him again. "The kiss doesn't matter." When his eyebrows rise, I rush to add, "I mean, it proved there's nothing between us."

"Ouch. Okay. I guess I should leave while I still have some of my pride left."

"That's not what I meant . . ."

He steps through the door then turns to meet my gaze. "Just for the record, I came with zero expectations. You're the one who made it awkward."

"Thanks for clarifying that." My tone is sharper than I mean for it to be, but I'm feeling like an asshole, and I want him to go.

He frowns again. "I'm not angry. I'm confused."

"Me too." I close the door in his face and sag back against it.

For someone so intelligent, you don't make smart decisions. My mother's words echo in my head because they fit this situation, as well as the one she called me about recently. Through her academic connections, she landed me an interview with a major pharmaceutical company. I could be putting my degree in biostatistics to use by researching how to cure diseases rather than wasting it analyzing financial trends for those who already have too much.

She made me promise to think about it and I did only because I wanted out of that conversation. I see a pattern in my behavior, and I don't like it. Sometimes it's like I'm two people . . . the one I feel like I should be and the other who sits back and marvels at all the stupid shit I do.

Greg is a good friend. I either should have told him everything or nothing. Dancing around the topic only made things worse.

I'll call him later and apologize. I'll tell him I started my period. If I'm lucky, he'll accept that as an excuse for my erratic behavior. I really enjoy my small circle of friends and don't want to lose them.

No wonder my parents are worried about me. When I imagined myself at this age, I thought I'd have my shit together.

I can't believe I fell for Mercedes' Project Inkwell story. My only consolation is that we all believed her. When she told me today Hugh was the one who told her the story and not the made-up uncle she claimed had, so much else made sense.

Hours of research had uncovered only rumors of Inkwell's existence. It was likely an urban legend soldiers created for entertainment—much like the wartime gremlin folklore. Somehow, Hugh heard about it and incorporated it into his fork fantasy. I admire his imagination, but that doesn't stop me from feeling foolish for spending so much time researching something that never happened.

Crossing the room to where I placed my purse earlier, I dig the spoon out and change my mind about returning it. Why do I need to put myself in another uncomfortable situation over this? If Mercedes wants her spoon back, let her ask me for it.

I open the junk drawer in my kitchen, toss the spoon in, and slam the drawer shut.

Done.

Not worth further thought or consideration.

Chapter Two

Jack

Boston, Massachusetts
1941

F EAR IS SOMETHING I've never allowed myself, but my heart is racing.

"There's still time to change your mind," my mother says as she parks the Plymouth Deluxe she taught herself to drive as soon as my father left for his latest deployment. Every able-bodied man is either already off to fight in the war, or they're readying themselves to go.

No one asks if I'll be called for duty. Many people's expectations of me lowered the day I was born and the doctor broke it to my parents that I was blind. My father fought the truth at first, summoning specialists from around the world. There was nothing any of them could do for me.

I died to him the day he accepted he couldn't fix me. He was a man used to being in control and my imperfection broke him on an elemental level. From that day onward, he claimed he didn't have a child—until my younger brother, Paul, was born.

Paul would be with Mom and me today, likely also trying to talk me out of this, if he wasn't already training to go. The irony of my father celebrating the son he adored heading overseas to fight in a war that so many were not returning from isn't lost on me.

Nor is the fact that I've asked the woman who has always protected me to give me the opportunity to do the same. I clear my throat. "You raised me to see beyond my limitations. If I can play a role, any role, in saving the world—I want to. No, I need to."

She places a hand over mine. "I know, but I wish Farley hadn't told you about the flier."

Farley is the only reason I feel I can leave her. I turn my hand so I can give hers a reassuring squeeze. He's been my mother's driver since before I was born. Now that the other male house staff have been called away to fight, he's taken on the role as general caretaker of the estate. In his late sixties, Farley is considered too old to serve, but I suspect he would have signed up anyway had he not felt my mother needed him.

He's always cared for the two of us. He was the one who secured tutors from Boston's school for the blind to educate me. He was the one who taught me martial arts and street fighting to ensure I can protect not only myself but my mother if I have to.

Although neither have ever said a word that hinted it, I suspect Farley loves my mother and would have stolen her from my father if he were younger. I wouldn't have judged him for it. Farley is a good man who believes I am as capable as any sighted person.

When he saw a flier with a fierce eagle descending for an attack, wings spread wide and proud, but with one leg instead of two, he thought of me. And then he shared the message:

Uncle Sam needs every bird in the air.

Support the troops by learning a specialized skill.

With your help, we will be invincible. Sign up today to save the world.

Farley knew it was an opportunity I couldn't pass by. Will it entail decoding encrypted messages? Going undercover to glean intel? We have no idea, but I have to do my part.

My mother is covertly as strong-willed as my father. She won't beg me to stay with her, just as she didn't ask my father or my brother to. This is a battle of good and evil. Everyone must do what they can. She'll let me go for the same reason she stays with my father: she believes it's her duty.

Still, I know it's not easy for her, so I raise a hand to locate her face then kiss her cheek. "Live or die, I do so unafraid. You made that possible and I love you for it."

Her hand finds mine again and she gives it a squeeze before saying, "When you exit the car, the flier says to go down an alley that is perpendicular to your side of the car. It's dimly lit so I'm not sure, but there doesn't appear to be anyone else here. The door you'll need to knock on will be on the right. If you'd like, I can walk you to—"

"No." I straighten, grab my walking stick, and open the car door. "And don't linger. It might not be safe. You should have allowed Farley to drive me."

Her voice has a familiar firmness when she says, "I will remain here for thirty minutes. If you do not return to tell me all is well, I have a revolver and I will go in there after you. I don't fear death either, not when it comes to my son." After a moment, she adds, "If this goes badly, and Farely had taken you I wouldn't be able to forgive him for it, and that wouldn't be fair to him."

"No, it wouldn't," I answer quietly. Integrity. Loyalty. Self-discipline. My mother has it all.

I could tell her not to risk her life to save mine, but I'd be wasting both of our time. Instead, I say, "I'll sign in, then I'll come back to tell you all is well."

Her deeply indrawn breath is audible and the only tell that her emotions are running high. "I understand why you can't sign up as a Chatfield, but thank you for honoring my family by using their surname."

"Jack Sully." I say the name aloud and like the way it sounds. *Less pretentious than Jackson Chatfield.* "It's a good name."

"A strong one."

I smile and unfold my large frame onto the sidewalk. "Move the car if you sense anything questionable. I'll find you."

"Be careful, Jackson—Jack." The slight crack in my mother's voice is my cue to leave.

"I will be," I say, despite knowing next to nothing about what I'm signing up for. The regular military branches are public, but none of them want me. I don't care who made those fliers, if they are offering people like me a chance to get involved and make a difference, I'll traverse a thousand musty alleys to meet with them.

Chapter Three

Cheryl

Providence, Rhode Island
2024

CLOSE MY eyes and let the warm water of the shower wash over my face. I've scrubbed every inch of my body and I still feel icky.

It's not that I don't know better than to go to a bar alone, but I was feeling down and . . . I don't know . . . maybe I'd wanted to prove something to myself. I wanted to be a strong, independent woman who ventured out into the world unafraid.

I shouldn't have accepted a drink from a man I didn't know, but the attention was welcome on a day when I was feeling low and looking for something to distract me. I'm not much of a drinker, so one can give me a buzz, but not with the punch that one did.

I knew instantly it was compromised.

When I said that loudly, Mr. Is-this-seat-taken-beautiful bolted.

Huge props to the bartender who believed me that I'd been slipped something. He had a taxi ready to take me to the hospital moments later. Nauseous but still somewhat clear-headed, I chose to be driven home.

A good decision? Probably not, but luckily, I live near the bar, and the full effect of what I was given is only now beginning to hit. I've already thrown up once. That's a good sign, isn't it? I wish it hadn't been right down the front of my dress, but at least I'm home.

And safe.

I think.

I leave the shower, stumble to the door of my apartment, and double-check that it's locked. There's a foul smell and I realize I didn't just throw up on myself but also on the nice beige carpeting of my living room.

I shake my head and feel a little dizzy as I do. Where's my phone? I should keep it close in case I feel worse.

If I pass out, I should definitely call 911.

I laugh at that thought as I stumble to the kitchen to get a bucket, gloves, and cleaning supplies. Then burst into tears. *There's nothing funny about this.*

On my hands and knees, I scrub the rug. As I finish, I spot another soiled area. If both the investment analysis gig and the pharmaceutical job fall through, I could be a professional projectile vomiter. The efficacy of my delivery to the largest area possible is impressive.

With a groan, I crawl around, cleaning more of the rug until I'm satisfied I've gotten it all. Only then do I remove my gloves and wipe the tears from my cheeks.

When I place my hands on my thighs as I struggle back to my feet, I realize I'm naked. I don't remember taking my clothes off. I do remember the vomit, though.

I should shower while I'm naked.

Didn't I just shower?

My hair is wet.

Oh, shit. I *did* shower. Am I getting dumber? What if I'm killing brain cells and come out of this dumb as a rock?

My parents will never forgive me.

But I might be too dumb to realize why they're upset.

That has me smiling.

I might end up blissfully, happily stupid.

No expectations.

I could just live my life, and that'd be enough.

My breasts jiggle as I move and I look down.

Why am I doing housework naked?

Why is the rug wet?

I scrubbed it.

Someone threw up.

Me.

As I strain to focus, I vaguely remember the bar and the trip home. I'm wasted, but I don't remember drinking a lot. But I must have.

And then I cleaned my house.

Naked.

I laugh then toss the cleaning supplies, including the soiled bucket, into the trash.

All gone.

That wasn't so bad.

Mid-yawn, I freeze. I'm not drunk, I was drugged.

I'm lucky to be alive.

What a fucking douchebag.

Someone needs to tell the police.

I should do that.

Tomorrow.

Fucking predator.

I should have dug my nails into his arm so I'd have some of his DNA.

Or kicked him in the balls.

Another wave of nausea rocks through me.

I'd better not die. I have to live long enough to make him suffer.

I need to make sure he doesn't do this to another woman.

Where's my phone? I could call now before I forget.

Did I take the phone into the shower with me?

I did shower, right?

I touch my wet hair.

Yep.

I did.

Oh, no. Not again.

This time I make it to the kitchen sink before I empty what little is left in my stomach.

I should call someone.

I can't call Greg. If he thought serving him beer was a come-on, meeting him at the door naked will definitely send the wrong message.

Ashley is on vacation.

I think.

Maybe she's back? I can't remember.

I can't call Mercedes. She might take this as an opportunity to pull me into her cutlery cult.

A laugh bursts from me at that.

Cutlery cult.

Kink.

Cutlery kink cult. That's not easy to say.

Kinky cutlery cult. Nope that's just as bad.

Another laugh escapes me.

Or good.

Who am I to judge?

I open my junk drawer and pull out the silver spoon I'd stashed there a week earlier.

Super soldier?

Right.

I wish.

Holding the spoon up to my face, I say, "If there's anyone in there, I've got a secret for you, but you can't tell anyone." The only sign of movement I see in the spoon is my distorted reflection, but I continue anyway. "I am a strong, independent woman, but sometimes I don't want to be the strong one. Tonight I did something stupid and I'm scared." Tears well in my eyes. "I know I'm not supposed to be scared. Women don't need men anymore. We don't need anyone. But I want someone to hold me and tell me everything is going to be okay. I want to curl up on the lap of someone who loves me just the way I am."

Sniffing, I mock the spoon. "Don't you dare judge me. I'm so sick of everyone telling me who I should be."

The spoon doesn't answer, but I don't expect it to. I continue, "If you really are trapped in there, you came to the wrong person, I don't believe in trying to change a man . . ."

Walking toward my bedroom, I joke, "Funny? Me? You think so? Sir, if you're complimenting me to get into my bed you are highly overestimating how difficult of a feat that is. I once fucked a guy only because I felt guilty about how expensive dinner was. I didn't even like the guy."

Pretending the spoon had responded in shock to that, I add, "It was only once, and the sex was disappointing, so you don't need to lecture me—lesson already learned."

A short time later, seated in the middle of my bed, still buck naked, still holding the damn silver spoon, I yawn and put it up near my face again. "You'll get used to being a spoon. I'm sure it's lonely in there, but guess what? People are lonely out here too. I couldn't wait to move out of my parents' house, but no one told me adulthood would mean spending so much time alone."

Still holding the spoon, I lay back against my pillows. "You're lucky you're a spoon. Stay that way. Life is hard." I sigh. "I feel like I have friends, but how many do I really have? I thought Greg was a friend, but now I think he only wants to fuck me. I thought life would get easier as I got older, but it's so fucking confusing. Staying home is lonely. Going out isn't safe. People suck." I wrinkle my nose. "You do too." I roll to my side and place the spoon on a spare pillow. "Stay there. I don't want to be alone if I wake up dead."

When the spoon remains as quiet as a spoon should, I close my eyes and turn away from it. "Even if there is a super soldier in you, I don't want him. It's not safe to want anyone. As soon as you open up to people, they either show you their crazy side or slip something in your drink. I can't let them win, though. Tomorrow, I'm going to the police about that guy at the bar and then I'm going to return you to Mercedes. And then we'll never speak of this day again."

Sleep comes while I'm trying to convince myself that I'm neither scared nor lonely.

Chapter Four

Jack

Lexington, Massachusetts
1942

I SHOULDN'T BE here, but when the alternative is one you can't live with, you do what you have to. My enhanced senses alert me of someone approaching, but it's my time as a blind person that allows me to quickly recognize the footsteps as Farley's.

Into the absolute darkness of a cloudy night, I whisper, "Farley, it's Jackson."

The footsteps stop, then hasten toward me and I'm engulfed in a hug from a man whose head just clears my shoulders. "It's been too long, Jackson. We began to fear for you."

I return the hug. "I'm okay. Actually, I'm better than okay. I can see now."

"What?" Despite the darkness, I can make out the details

of Farley's face. Long and thin, just like the rest of him. His hair is white and slicked back, but his eyes are as kind as I've always imagined they'd be. I fight back the urge to hug him again. This is who I think of when someone asks me about my father. "How is that possible?"

"I can tell you everything I know, but I don't have much time. I've already put you and Mom at risk by coming here. Something will happen soon that will make it impossible for me to come home again, at least until after the war, but I couldn't leave without—"

"Seeing your mother's face."

He knows me well. I swallow the emotion that momentarily clogs my throat. "I'm determined to come back, Farley, but just in case I don't . . ."

He nods.

"There's also something I need to say. They know who I am and who my father is. They let me register as Jack Sully, but it didn't change the requirement put on every man in the program. Jackson Chatfield must die before we deploy. It'll be an accident and the body that's found will be damaged beyond recognition. It won't be me, but it needs to be accepted and buried as me."

"Your mother—"

"That's why I'm here. I couldn't leave knowing she'd be mourning something that didn't happen. I'll be honest with you, what I'm doing is dangerous. I might not be back, but I'll die a hero . . . just not doing whatever they say happened."

"I don't understand any of this. How did they fix your eyesight?"

"They're giving us injections." I shrug and sigh. "Not everyone survives them, but if you do, it fixes whatever is wrong with you. More than fixes it. I'm getting stronger every day and if I get hurt, I heal faster than normal. Really fast. And severed parts regenerate."

He gasps. "What in God's name have they done to you?" He mutters a prayer beneath his breath.

"I don't believe this has anything to do with God, but then, I don't think war ever does. There are rumors the British Royal Air Force plans to increase bombing raids and target Cologne. They want us well planted before that happens."

"The British?"

"No, Project Inkwell. I work for them. I'm a soldier, but not technically enlisted."

"I don't like the sound of that. And how do you know that what they're doing to you is safe?"

I laugh without humor. "Are any of us safe? Will any of us ever be again if we don't fight for what we have?" The attack on Pearl Harbor had shown us that we couldn't sit back and remain uninvolved. We were in the fight already and we were determined to win it.

"So they're sending you into battle?"

"They say we'll be doing something even more important

than fighting in the trenches. I won't have a way to send news home for a while, but if I'm able to, I'll sign it J. Sully."

"Farley?" my mother's voice calls out through the night.

Farley and I walk out of the shadows and toward the porch my mother is standing on. When she sees me, she runs down the steps and right into my arms. "You're alive," she murmurs again and again.

"I am." I lift her off her feet in a tight hug.

When I put her down, I meet her gaze and her hand flies to her mouth in shock. "You can see me?"

Emotion blurs my now perfect vision. "I can."

Her hands cup my face, pulling it down and closer to hers. "Your eyes are a different color."

"Yes, but now they work."

Tears flow down her cheeks, but she's smiling. "My boy. I'm so happy for you."

I lay my hands over hers. "There are things we need to discuss, Mom, and my time is severely limited."

She sniffs, wipes both of her cheeks, then motions for us to follow her into the house. In the sitting room, Farley, my mother, and I share a moment of silence when I finish retelling as much as I felt my mother could handle. I didn't share how many men had died from the injections or how horrific their deaths were. I kept to the facts that would comfort her.

"Should I tell Paul?" she asks.

I shake my head. "This is the kind of program that must

remain under the radar to be effective. I wouldn't have told you, but I didn't want you to receive erroneous news of my death."

Chin high, hands clasped on her lap, my mother accepts what must sound like an outlandish and perilous path to choose. If she disapproves, there's no sign of it in her expression. Being married to my father has taught her to conceal her feelings on most matters.

I glance back and forth between her and Farley and for a moment wish my mother had chosen someone like him. Farley's attentiveness to my mother's needs and appreciation of her strength are unfaltering. He looks at her like there is no one and nothing more important to him . . . and it's as beautiful a sight to witness as it is melancholy. She deserves better than my father, but she'll never leave him.

I sigh.

There are things within my control and things that are not. "They say we'll be able to come home after the war. If I have a breath left in me, this isn't goodbye. I'll be back."

Her forehead furrows. "As Jack Sully?"

"As whoever I'm allowed to be."

She presses her lips together then says, "I'll ensure there is something for you when you return."

"Mom, you don't have to—"

"Jackson—Jack, you'll need resources. You're different now and people won't accept that easily. Coming back here may not be possible for you. Unless you can pretend to be blind again. It's better to be prepared and underestimated than to stand out and invite the wrath of those stronger than you."

Was that how she felt about my father? My fists clenched at my sides. If he ever laid a hand on her it would be the last thing he did before meeting his creator. When I return, and I will, I'll build a home as grand as my father's and give my mother a safe place where she can be as outspoken as she pleases. "I'll be careful, and I'll be back."

She walks over and looks me in the eye. "Don't forget to be kind as well. You've always had a good heart. No matter how strong they make you or how this war goes, don't let anyone take that from you."

Chapter Five

Cheryl

Providence, Rhode Island
2024

A s I step into the elevator at Mercedes' apartment building, I'm still hungover, but the police said that's normal. They also said I should be checked out by a doctor, but that would require rehashing what I did the night before again, and I want to put the experience behind me. The police have a description of the man who slipped something into my drink, and they say they'll track him down.

I don't want to think about it anymore.

One painfully awkward conversation down; one to go.

With morning came some clarity. The creep at the bar was dangerous, but Mercedes was harmless. I overreacted when I ran from her. What I should have done was calmly hand the spoon back to her, thank her for the offer, and politely decline it.

And that's what I intend to do.

I text Mercedes to make sure she is home.

She is.

Hugh is too, but that doesn't matter. He has also never been anything but friendly toward me. So they like to role-play. That's their business. All I have to do is express I'm not interested and we can all go back to how things were before.

No harm done.

Sporting an excited smile, Mercedes swings her door open and looks around as if expecting someone to be with me. When she notes that I'm alone, she cocks her head to one side and beckons me inside.

Hugh rises from the couch to greet me from across the room. Had he approached me, I might have run again, and he appears to sense that. "Hi, Cheryl."

My voice comes out strangled. "Hi." I jump at the sound of Mercedes closing the door.

When she joins me, I try to discreetly put space between us by sidestepping like I've seen royals do in videos. I clear my throat then say, "I'm here to return the spoon."

"Return?" Disappointment darkens Mercedes eyes.

I dig the spoon out of my purse then hold it toward her. "I shouldn't have taken it. Whatever the two of you are into is your business and I'm not judging, but it's not for me."

Mercedes accepts the spoon with a frown. "You don't feel anything for it?"

A blush warms my cheeks as I remember waking up with

it on the pillow beside me. "No, but I'm not into cutlery." There, that's as clear as it gets.

Pursing her lips, Mercedes glances at Hugh. "I felt an instant connection to you when you were a fork. Do you think it has to be a love match to work?"

I gurgle with a laugh that takes me by surprise. They have love matches with their silverware? What are they doing with their utensils? I fan my face. I don't want to know. I wince. Doesn't it hurt? No, I need to stop imagining this. I take a step toward the door. "Mercedes, I've enjoyed getting to know you . . . and the two of you seem like a great couple. I think, though, for us to remain friends, we should have boundaries about what we share. I don't need . . . or want . . . to hear about your sex life."

"We need to show her, Mercedes," Hugh says.

I raise both hands. "No. No. This is what I'm talking about. You don't need to *show* me anything. I'm not interested."

"Do it," Mercedes says.

There's a quick flash and a fork clatters to the floor. Hugh is gone. I snap my head around looking for him, but there's no sign of him.

They're into magic as well?

Mercedes walks over to the fork, but before she reaches it her cat bats it under the couch. "Mike, you know that's naughty!" She drops to her knees to reach for the fork.

Her feral feline stares me down as if expecting me to take

his side. I look away and shift awkwardly from one foot to another.

Rump in the air, her voice is muffled as she twists and stretches for the fork. "Hugh says cats don't like the paranormal. They sense when something isn't right."

There's a lot for Mike to sense in this situation, but I keep that thought to myself.

"Got it." Mercedes turns and rises to her feet with the fork in one hand and the spoon in another. When she sees my expression, she says, "How could you still not believe me? You just saw Hugh become a fork."

"I saw something." Where is Hugh? Hiding in another room?

She waves the fork at me. "*This* is Hugh."

I raise my hands as a sign of surrender and back away. "I believe that you believe that's Hugh."

She sighs. "It's a lot. I know. In the beginning, I kept thinking I'd lost my mind . . . that I was dreaming."

"If it's any consolation, that was an impressive illusion."

"It wasn't a trick. Hugh is in this fork. Someone trapped him in there. They trapped his whole unit in cutlery. You have to believe me. They are war heroes and now they need our help."

Rubbing a hand over my forehead, I wonder if I'm still at home and this is a drug-induced dream. I tell myself to wake up and imagine a door I can walk through to leave the dream. It was a method my mother taught me as a young child when I suffered from recurring nightmares. It had worked well back then.

It doesn't work this time.

Fuck, this is real.

"I don't know what this is, Mercedes, but I wish only the best for both you and Hugh," I say, taking another step toward the door.

She rushes to my side. "I'd show you the fork becoming Hugh again but that still requires me . . . us . . . mutually pleasuring each other."

"Us?" As in me and her? Oh, hell, no. "Sorry, I'm not into anything like that."

"Not you. Me and Hugh." Her smile is so amused and unthreatening I wonder if this is a prank. "It's the only way to bring him back."

I nod. She doesn't seem like she's joking. "That's . . . that's . . ." I should have washed the spoon before I put it in my purse. Eww.

Mercedes frowns. "You didn't feel *any* connection with the spoon?"

I glance around. If she's filming this, she's hidden the camera well. "Sorry, nothing." I speak clearly in case I am being recorded.

"I don't get it," she mutters, then looks down at the spoon. Her mouth rounds. "Wait. There's no scar."

I make a face and retreat another step. She closes the distance between us. "Look at Hugh's fork." She shows me a mark on the back of it then holds up the spoon. "Now look at the spoon. Nothing. Zero marks. Maybe there's no one in this one."

"No one in it," I echo. Okay, this is going on too long to be a skit to share online. She's definitely struggling with reality.

"Come with me," she commands and begins to walk toward her kitchen.

"No." I'm done.

She looks over her shoulder. "*Please.* This will all make sense if you let me show you something."

I do want something to make sense today so I follow her to the place in her kitchen where she keeps a wooden box of silverware. Please let this be where she tells me all of this is an elaborate joke.

After placing the silverware on the counter, she opens the box labeled Inkwell. She removes several pieces and lays them side by side. "Hugh said there were twelve remaining men in his unit. There are more pieces of silverware than that in here. It makes sense that some would have nothing in them." She examines each piece, front and back, then sorts them into two piles. "These are unmarked. These all have etchings on them."

A quick look confirms that some have marks, and others do not—not that that signifies anything of importance. Mercedes had me fooled at first, but since she confessed that she lied about having an uncle who told her about Project

Inkwell, I have reason to doubt everything she says. Hugh is in on that lie, too. Hugh, the man who claims he transforms into a fork.

Mercedes holds up a spoon. "Oh, my God, this one has two dots on the front. I wonder if it's Jack. He was born blind. Hugh describes him as loyal to his core. A good, good man." She turns the spoon and sees a line near the end of the handle. "He also lost a leg in an explosion."

I gasp. Not because I believe her, but because I've watched war documentaries and injuries like that are horrific.

"Don't worry," she reassures me, "it grew back. As long as they're alive, these men regenerate."

Mouth dry, I mutter, "Because they're super soldiers."

"Yes," she answers enthusiastically. "You have no idea how happy Hugh will be if we bring his best friend back." She offers the spoon to me. "Hold it. Tell me if you feel a connection."

"No." Their tale of super soldiers and government secret projects is impressively detailed, but I shouldn't get further involved.

Still holding it out to me, Mercedes searches my face. "Do you *want* to be single?"

"What kind of question is that?" I wince.

"Have you ever met someone online?"

"Sure."

"Been on a blind date?"

I reluctantly nod.

"So you're open to meeting someone in unusual ways and willing to take a chance, but not do this."

I place a hand on one hip. "It's hardly the same thing."

"You're right. Anyone can meet someone online. You're being offered a chance to rescue a man who will adore you for it. A good, loyal, loving man."

"Please stop. I've heard enough."

"It's okay to have reservations about this. In fact, I'd worry about you if you didn't." An encouraging smile spreads across her face. "But imagine having a Hugh of your own. Jack is tall. He towers over Hugh. A gentle giant. Kind. Strong. Hugh says Jack is an optimist. A family man. Sounds like someone who's worth taking a leap of faith for."

Tempting as the idea of magically summoning the perfect man sounds, things like that are not scientifically feasible. "You should be an author—fantasy seems to be your forte."

"I'm not claiming to understand how or why this works, but I believe Hugh and I were meant to be. Jack might be in this spoon and not respond to you at all because you may not be who he's meant for." Mercedes steps closer. "But what if he's in there waiting for *you*. You could free him. All I'm asking you to do is hold the spoon. If you don't feel anything, you can go and I'll never talk about silverware with you again."

"Never?" If she tucked her crazy back in, that would solve a lot of problems. I frown. "This is it. You won't ask me to touch any of the other silverware?"

"You have my word."

"All I have to do is hold it?"

"Yes. And think about how nice it would be to meet someone who still believes in love, loyalty, and happily ever after."

I blink a few times quickly. "I don't believe in any of that. Not anymore."

"Just take the spoon and keep an open mind."

I suppose there's no risk and she promised to not bring this topic up again if it doesn't work. I'll hold the spoon, make a wish, verify that nothing happens, hand it back, and we'll be done.

As soon as the spoon touches my skin, I feel the difference between it and the other spoon. It quickly warms to the heat of my hand. My fingers close around it and the oddest sensations curl through me.

The marks on it are beautiful.

I was meant to have this spoon.

It's mine.

Confused, I meet Mercedes' gaze. "Are you hypnotizing me or something?"

Her smile widens. "You feel it, don't you? The connection. The warmth. It's confusing and scary, but it means this will work this time."

My heart is racing as I proclaim, "I'm not fucking a spoon."

Mercedes holds out her hand. "Okay, then give it back."

My fingers tighten on the handle of it. "No."

Turning, Mercedes picks up the fork she claims is Hugh and hugs it to her chest. "There's no rush. Relationships need to unfold. Take the spoon home. Get to know it. When the time is right . . . things will just happen."

I look at the spoon in my hand and tell myself to give it back before it's too late. My parents will have me committed if I tell them I even entertained the idea of being intimate with a utensil.

The problem is, I don't want to give the spoon back. The way my sex is tingling with an inexplicable anticipation is terrifying, but also exciting.

Ushering me out the door of her apartment, Mercedes says, "Now, I don't mean to be rude, but I'd like to tell Hugh what happened and I'd rather no one else be here while I bring him back."

She closes the door in my face, and I stand there, clutching the spoon in one hand.

Is insanity catching? I'd told myself I wanted nothing to do with Mercedes and Hugh's silverware kink, but I can't deny how good the spoon feels in my hand.

Would it feel as good on other parts of me?

My breath catches. No, I did not just imagine myself fucking a spoon—and liking it.

I stash it in my purse and head to the elevator. The whole way to my house I reassure myself all I experienced was the power of suggestion. Even otherwise-sensible people spot the Loch Ness monster if they are prepped with enough stories about it.

That's all this is.

I'm lonely and Mercedes sold me a fairy tale that hit close enough to what I've been craving that my mind wants to accept it.

I'm too smart to fall for something like that.

Back in my apartment, I remove the spoon from my purse and hold it over my open junk drawer. The two marks on the bowl of it catch my attention. What had Mercedes said? The marks represent scars? Jack's eyes?

He was born blind? That must have been hard for him.

I shake my head. There *is* no Jack.

This is a spoon.

Mercedes and Hugh did some kind of disappearing magic trick to fool me.

People don't become trapped in cutlery.

Not even super soldiers.

Because there is no such thing as a super soldier.

I close the junk drawer without placing the spoon in it. There is something different about this spoon. What would it hurt to study it?

With warm water and soap, I wash it in the sink. As I do, I run my fingers up and down the length of it and shudder at how erotic the action feels. I've slept with men who didn't turn me on this much.

This is wrong.

I place the spoon on the dish rack beside the sink and force myself to walk away from it. In the living room, I take out my laptop and read the job description I received for the position at the pharmaceutical company. If I am as intelligent as my parents think I am, maybe it's time to start making smarter decisions.

An ad for silverware pops up on my feed, and I hastily close it like it's porn.

Chapter Six

Jack

Providence, Rhode Island
2024

T HERE'S NOTHING . . . then there's her.

I wonder if I'm dead and in heaven. I'm surrounded by the scent and taste of a woman. Her presence provides warmth and comfort, then ignites an intense yearning.

Wherever I am feels temporary. Is this woman, or essence of a woman, what will guide me to the light? If so, I'll go eagerly.

I didn't anticipate the afterlife being so . . . sexual. Maybe it's whatever people want it to be. God knows, it's been a long time since I've been with a woman.

Not that I've been with many. It was difficult to meet them when my father hid me away at every social event. My first lover was a divorced woman who was hired to teach me biology. Some might argue that she did . . . but with a more hands on approach than expected with a focus on the human reproductive organs.

The next woman I was with had arranged to meet me through Farley. He'd said he didn't approve of her, but I liked her—at first, anyway. She was funny and wickedly flirtatious, not as good in the sack as my tutor, but more than willing . . . until she discovered my father hadn't included me in his will.

Another woman sought me out when the war first started. I suspect she knew my father and brother would deploy and if they didn't return, I might inherit by default. She was cunning but not bright enough to realize that being blind didn't mean I was uneducated. I quickly lost interest in her.

I thought I must be hideous, but after joining Project Inkwell and regaining my sight, I saw my face for the first time. My jaw is square. My head is covered with a healthy amount of hair. Few men I encounter are as tall or as muscled. Women give me long, bold looks that even a previously blind man knows how to interpret.

I came to Inkwell already in fighting shape. Farley's philosophy was that nearly anyone, sighted or not, could be taken down by a fast fist. He also taught me to hone my senses until I could not only recognize someone's presence but also track and anticipate their movements through sound and vibration.

My handlers at Inkwell closely monitored how the injections affected my already fine-tuned senses. I wouldn't say I can hear, see, taste, smell, or feel any better than the other men in my unit, but I can isolate desired stimuli and block out the extraneous. Add increased speed and my ability to move around people without being noticed and I can become virtually invisible—no easy feat for a man who's closer to seven than six feet tall.

Is?

Was?

Am I still me or something else?

Who is this woman whose touch envelops me? There is no escaping the way she strokes the length of me. Although I can't see her, this is nothing like being blind. I'm here, but not. She is both with me and in some far-off place.

I'm hers to do with as she pleases.

Up and down, she strokes me until I'm nearly out of my mind. Unable to speak, but craving more of her so intensely that if I could utter any words, they would be: *Don't stop.*

She does, though, and I'm gutted by the absence of her.

Alone in the nothingness, I scream but am unable to make a sound.

This isn't heaven.

It's hell.

And I'm trapped.

Chapter Seven

Cheryl

Providence, Rhode Island
2024

THE LINE TO get into my favorite breakfast diner is out the door, but that's because its "Specials" board is always full of decadent, gourmet creations that people drive from all around Rhode Island to experience. The front of the restaurant is in an unassuming old-style diner car that still has counter service on red stools that spin, as well as booths that look like they haven't changed since the 1950s. "I'm getting the matcha souffle pancakes," I announce.

My friend Ashley chuckles. "You had that last week. Try something different."

The line moves forward a few feet. "I know what I like."

"Yes, but there's something to be said for expanding your palate and trying something new. Look at me and Leo. If we never got drunk and accidentally had sex, we might not be dating now. We wouldn't have just had an amazing vacation."

An older woman behind us makes a tsk sound in judgment. Ashley's cheeks go pink and I'm tempted to ream out our eavesdropper, but a better idea comes to me. I nod toward the woman behind us then wink at Ashley. "Would you share him?"

"Share? With you?" Ashley asks with a twinkle in her eye. *Game on.*

I sigh dramatically. "I don't have time for a boyfriend. I just want to fuck someone."

The woman behind us gasps and whispers to the person behind her, "Did you hear that?"

Pretending to be unaware that our conversation isn't private, Ashley says, "As long as you like anal, sure. That's all he wants to do. Anal. Anal. Anal. I'm so damn stretched out he needs to start using his fist."

"Sounds like you should share some of that goodness," I joke. "Does he have a friend? I haven't been in a threesome since last summer. Unless appliances count—do they? The things I've done with my blender should be illegal."

"Oh, my God," the woman screeches. "You're both disgusting."

Ashley turns and flashes a toothy smile at her. "The last woman who called me a name spent a month in a collar up at my cabin in Maine. I had to free her, even though she begged to stay at the end. Are you into that?"

"I'm not listening to another moment of this," the older woman proclaims as she grabs the arm of the man with her and storms away. He doesn't look as eager to leave, but he goes with her.

Before they're out of earshot, both Ashley and I burst out laughing. After catching my breath, I say, "First, now I know we're reading all the same books. Second, we're going to hell for that."

Shamelessly, she shrugs. "At least we'll be with all of our friends." She glances at the woman who is storming across the parking lot. "She deserved that. Everyone knows when you're listening to a conversation you're not in, proper etiquette requires you pretend you can't hear it."

"Yeah. You and I should open an etiquette school. We're proper alright."

"Those who love us, accept us. Those who don't, don't matter."

She's right. "Can you imagine how many people she's going to tell about this?"

"We'll live rent-free in her head for weeks . . . possibly months."

I chuckle. "I wonder if she'll google wearing a collar."

"If she does all her ads will reflect where her curiosity takes her."

"Sometimes I wish more old people knew how to use TikTok. We're in rare form today. I feel like we could have made her account blow up."

We're both still smiling when the line moves forward again. "Back to what we were talking about; I had a really good time with Leo. We should go on a double date."

"Except for the small detail of me not dating anyone."

She makes a face. "What about Greg?"

I shake my head. "I'm not interested in him."

"Have you given him a shot?"

I remember how I felt nothing when Greg suggested that we fuck and see how it goes, and it makes me a little sad. He's a nice guy with a job and an apartment. He's not even bad looking. We have the same friends—the same interests. On paper, he makes sense. I wish I felt something for him. I've never tasted cardboard, but I know it wouldn't tantalize my tastebuds. I feel the same way about getting Greg naked. "If you're suggesting I accidentally sleep with him to see if it changes how I feel, let me remind you that you liked Leo before you got drunk with him."

We give our names to a hostess who tells us we have another few minutes before we'll be seated. We tell her that's fine. We wouldn't have chosen this place if we were in a hurry.

We're corralled with a group of people off to one side of the doorway. Ashley lowers her voice. "My feelings for Leo were a surprise to me."

"Not to me. He's all you've talked about for the last month. Ever since you helped him paint his garage."

"That was a fun day." She wrinkles her nose at me.

"There are things I've always liked about him, but I didn't think he was hot until . . . I probably shouldn't share the details."

"Don't hold back, but do speak up," a man off to one side says. My eyebrows shoot up when I realize he and the woman beside him look like they're in their eighties. She has a walker. He has a cane. He's bald with ridiculously large white eyebrows that perfectly match her wild head of white curls.

"Harold, stop." The older woman bats his arm playfully. "He's hoping you'll try to scare him off with more smut talk. You had his attention at anal. I promised him if we both make it to his one hundredth birthday that's the present he'll get. He's spent the last fifty years reminding me of that promise." She rolls her eyes. "The old bastard plans to hang around just for that."

"Damn right," her husband says proudly. "Twelve years, seven months, and ten days to go."

"Oh, Lord," she says, but she hugs his arm. "I'd leave you right now, but I don't think I can outrun you anymore."

"You never could." He puts that arm around her and kisses her on the cheek.

The look she gives him is all love. "You know I never tried."

As the couple temporarily forgets about us and loses themselves in each other's eyes, I link arms with Ashley. "If I don't find something that good, I'm staying single."

Ashley adds, "I'd tell you that your standards are too high, but I agree. I want that too."

A name is called, and the couple shuffles away.

After a brief silence, I ask, "Do you think you and Leo could get serious?"

The pause before she answers is telling. "I don't know. I like him—a lot. He's super sweet. He'll pick his underwear up off the bathroom floor and put it in the hamper, but I don't know if that's enough. Maybe it's outdated . . . or a result of reading too many dark romances . . . but I want someone who'll not just love me, but protect me. I want to know he'd kill for me, die for me . . ."

"I think the men we lust over in books wouldn't translate to good husbands. Do you really want someone you have to visit in prison because he offs every man who looks at you?"

Ashley sighs. "I don't want him to kill anyone . . . I only need to believe he would. I'd bury anyone beneath a shed in my backyard if they ever came for the people I love. All I want is someone who'd do the same for me."

I slip my arm out of hers and wrinkle my nose at her. "Those are the kind of intrusive thoughts you shouldn't share out loud . . . and never put them online. You don't want to limit your career choices."

She rolls her eyes at me. "Sometimes when you speak I know exactly what your parents said to you growing up."

"Ouch." What puts a real sting to her words is how right she is. "That's actually word for word what my mother has said." I smile at the irony of it. "I need to tuck that side of me back in."

She smiles. "It's good to be cautious as long as you don't let it hold you back. Like your job. Do you even enjoy it? I never hear you talk about it."

"It's work. Am I supposed to love it?"

"I enjoy my job."

"That's because you work for a robotics start up and they're convinced they couldn't exist without you."

Her smile is genuine and pleased. "I do contribute to the process. I was supposed to oversee development, but now I have my own mini-lab. It's so cute. I tinker all day with all sorts of materials, testing them for durability on tiny proto-types. When I'm bored, I design clothing for them even though they're not humanoids. It's the fucking funniest thing. Mark my word, no matter how many arms we give them, robot clothing will be a big market in the future, and I'll have my finger on the pulse of what they like."

"Wow. Okay. Back to you and Leo," I joke. The idea of robots having a preference for clothing gives me the creeps.

"Whatever. All I'm saying is that you need to find some-thing you love. Have you looked into the job your parents suggested?"

"I will."

"The only thing worse than being wrong is being indeci-sive."

"Now you sound like my mother."

"Ouch," she says with a laugh. "Sorry."

"No, you're right. One way or another I need to make a decision." And this is why we're friends. We're real with each other even when it's uncomfortable. Ashley's the type who will not just answer a 3:00 a.m. phone call, but will immediately jump into her car and come over if she thinks a friend is in need. She doesn't sugar coat her opinions, but I don't need her to. I love our friendship the way it is. "Hey, I have a question . . . a scenario to run by you."

"Regarding Greg?"

"No." I rub a hand over my forehead and ask myself if I really want to open a conversation on a ridiculous topic. "Mercedes Hopper."

"Greg's friend. The weird one."

I nod. From the first time Greg introduced Mercedes to our group, we liked her, but it was clear she had little in common with us. She is nice, though, and so grateful to have friends that we felt we had to accept her. "She's engaged."

"No." Ashley's mouth rounds in shock.

"Yes."

"When—how—tell me everything."

"His name is Hugh. She originally told me they'd dated in the past and they'd gotten back together when he returned to town."

"You don't believe her?"

I chew my bottom lip. "I don't know what to believe anymore. Remember everything she told us about Project

Inkwell?"

"Of course. That was a fun rabbit hole to go down."

"It was all a lie. She and Hugh came up with the story."

"Oh. Well, shit. That's disappointing. And not entirely true. There was something called Project Inkwell."

I purse my lips briefly. "Maybe. Maybe not. I didn't find anything more concrete than chatter about it. You?"

"Rumors." She shakes her head. "What a bummer. I'm sure our government did some sick things back then, and I don't condone any of it, but the idea of them creating super soldiers was kind of exciting."

"I thought so as well and that's proof that we've watched way too many superhero movies."

"So, is Mercedes out of the friend group?"

I shrug. "I don't know. I'm not sure she can help herself. I'll be nice to her, but I wouldn't take another research idea from her."

"Nor would I."

"She also told me a few things that she asked me not to tell other people."

Ashley does a quick scan of the room then leans toward me. "As your best friend, I don't classify as other people. Anything you tell me goes into a vault I take with me to my grave."

"A little dramatic, but I do trust you."

"As you should. Now spill."

"I feel bad already and I haven't even said it yet. Is that a sign that I should keep it to myself?"

"I guess it depends on what it's about. If someone hurt her and she's battling shame—yeah, don't tell me that stuff. But if she was raised on a clown commune and her first language was mime—you can't keep that kind of shit to yourself."

"A clown commune?" I choke on a laugh. "Where do you come up with this stuff?"

She shrugs. "My mind works in mysterious ways. Okay, so, are you going to tell me or what?"

In that moment I realize Ashley and I might be as odd as Mercedes is. I don't know how I feel about that. "Mercedes' fiancé believes he was part of a government testing program." When Ashley's expression doesn't register the shock I thought it might, I realize I left off the most important part. "During World War II."

Ashley blinks a few times quickly. "So, he's mentally unwell? That's sad."

"He has to be, right?" I clear my throat. "He doesn't just *believe* he was experimented on back then, he also thinks he was made into some kind of super soldier and then—"

"Then?" She leans closer. When I give her a look, her eyes widen and her grin is unapologetic. "What? I live on the conspiracy theory side of TikTok—purely for entertainment purposes."

I shake my head. "This is serious."

"Great, because I'm seriously dying to hear what else he

believes."

Whatever. "He said the government turned him and his unit into silverware."

The choked laughter Ashley lets out perfectly reflects how I felt when I first heard the story. "That's awesome."

I'd be laughing along if I hadn't spent the last week feeling oddly attached to a spoon. "A fork. He thinks he spent the last eighty years as a fork."

"What a great way to get rid of a super soldier while letting them remain useful."

"You're not taking this seriously."

Her face contorts as she attempts to stop smiling. "I need to know how he became a man again."

Beneath my breath, I mumble, "She was intimate with him."

"What did you say?"

After clearing my throat again, I raise my voice slightly. "I'm not sure exactly what the process entailed, but Mercedes had sex with the fork and that brought Hugh back."

Ashley is now gurgling on laughter and I get it. It's a preposterous story. "I love everything about this. Mercedes can't leave our friend group. I need to hear this story from her."

"You don't think she's delusional?"

"Oh, she's bonkers, but so are you . . . and so am I. Do both she and Hugh believe this?"

"Yes."

"They say every pot has a lid. I'm glad she found hers. Are they happy?"

"Yes. Very much so."

Ashley wipes at the corner of her eyes. "That's all that matters."

"I guess."

"A fork." She laughs again. "Do you think they use utensils in the bedroom as part of their fantasy? Sounds forking painful."

I roll my eyes. "I didn't ask too many questions."

"Are you kidding? How can you not want to know *everything* about this? I'm fascinated. Did he believe he was a fork before he met her? Is this a fantasy they came up with together? Is this something only they do, or is there a subculture of people diddling cutlery? I have questions. So many questions. And the tines . . . ouch."

"I'm sure they use the other end."

"How sure? What did they say?"

I close my eyes for a moment and shake my head. "They didn't say and I didn't ask."

"I forking would have."

That gets a chuckle out of me. "You're having a lot of fun with this."

"And wondering why you're not."

The hostess calls out my name and announces that our table is ready. I motion for us to go. Ashley falls into step beside me.

Once we're both seated, she unwraps her silverware from the napkin it's tucked in. With a huge smile, she holds up a fork. "Imagine if the world actually worked that way? Hello, there Mr. Fork. Are you a man from the 1940s? What's that?" She holds the fork to her ear then laughs flirtatiously. "Not on the first date. Okay, just this once. And only my mouth."

I groan into my hand. All of what she's saying would be hilarious if I wasn't holding back a confession of my own. I unwrap my own silverware and touch it tentatively, afraid I'll feel a connection to one of them . . . while also worrying that I won't. The stainless steel is cold and lifeless. As it should be.

With a huge smile, Ashley places the fork back on the table. "Thank you. I needed this."

"Tough week?"

Some of her smile fades. "No. Just a little confusing. I like Leo. I do. I don't know . . ."

I nod without commenting because I've been there.

We're interrupted long enough to give our drink and food order. Ashley waits until we're alone again before she says, "Enough about me. I need to know if they sent you home with a fork of your own . . ."

"A spoon," I say in a thick voice.

Her face lights up with delight. "You're serious."

"Yes. And that's not the worst part."

"You fucked it."

"No."

Her lips purse. "You want to fuck it?"

When I don't immediately deny that, her mouth drops open. "I'm not going to do it," I say in a rush. "It's just weird to feel something for an inanimate object." I lean forward and whisper, "How much it yearns to be free." Do I dare? "And to be with me."

Her eyes round. "There's a super soldier trapped in the spoon Mercedes gave you and he wants to *be* with you?"

I shouldn't admit something like this aloud. I shouldn't even allow myself to think it. "I don't know what's in that spoon. All I know is I can't stop thinking about it and when I hold it . . ."

Ashley bits her bottom lip. "Yes?"

I grimace. "I want to believe someone is in there and I can free him."

She puts up a hand in a quiet request for a moment. "I love this for you, but I'm also a little worried that you're not joking."

I sound crazy.

I know I do.

But that doesn't change how I feel.

I say, "Jack Sully is the name of the soldier Mercedes thinks in trapped in the spoon. He's kind, tall, devoted to his family . . ." God, I've lost my mind.

Her expression turns sympathetic. "My brother is still single if you're lonely."

I shake my head.

"You're in a relationship slump. If you want, I'm willing to watch some woman on woman porn with you to see if expanding your options is something you're open to."

I frown, wonder if that means what I think it means, shake my head, and say, "Thanks, but I don't think I'm interested in women."

"Just cutlery?" she taunts gently. When I don't immediately say anything, she adds, "Sorry. This was funny when it was about Mercedes. I've known you long enough to know this isn't like you. You should probably give Mercedes a little space."

Our food is delivered to our table, but neither of us makes a move to touch it. "You think she's messing with my head?"

"I think you're looking for something to distract yourself from the decisions you don't want to make."

I nod. That makes sense and fills me with some relief. I've put off making any kind of decision about the job my parents arranged for me to have a shot at. The mind is a funny thing. When a person doesn't want to do something, it'll create all kinds of excuses. "Okay, last question, before we drop this topic for today."

"Okay."

"If you thought there was the slightest chance that being intimate with a utensil would result in the man of your dreams appearing, would you . . .?"

Ashley gives me a long look, then a slow smile. "Love is love and what happens in the privacy of your kitchen . . ."

"Jerk." I smile back. "At least a spoon isn't dangerous."

"Leo would be a spoon." She laughs then some of the light leaves her eyes. "A teaspoon."

"I don't want Leo."

Ashley purses her lips. "I'm not sure I do either. I liked being with him, but I think I want to go back to being friends. He doesn't get my humor. I need someone with a little edge to him."

"Perhaps someone with a sharp tongue like yours?" I say with growing humor. "Someone who can cut through your bullshit?"

She waves a finger at me. "If you show up at my door with a knife—"

"I promise I won't . . ." I wiggle my eyebrows at her. "Unless I have a man named Jack with me."

"Oh, my God." She leans back and smiles. "That would be amazing."

"All joking aside, if you were me, would you try it . . . just once . . . just to see?"

Chapter Eight

Jack

Providence, Rhode Island
2024

WHY COME TO me only to withdraw again?

Why torment me by waking me, then leave me in this place with only my thoughts and an aching need for you?

Did I earn this hell?

Flashes of my last memories taunt me. I'm at an award ceremony in London celebrating my unit's many successful missions. We're receiving medals to honor the role we played in stopping Germany from creating a weapon of mass destruction.

The war is over—at least with Germany. We're euphoric.

Ray is being the louse he often is. I know he can't help himself. From the little he's told us of his life before joining Inkwell, it's easy to understand why he trusts very few people and often pushes away those who would help him.

He and I became close. Ironically, it was just after he brought a knife to what should have been a hand-to-hand-combat sparring session. With a viciousness that took the rest of us by surprise, he'd stabbed Hugh and nearly killed him.

Boldly.

Defiantly.

The senselessness of almost ending Hugh infuriated me, as did his stance that he'd done it to remind all of us that war doesn't play by any man's rules. If we were to survive, he reminded us to trust no one—not even each other.

Still, I sought him out afterward. What I'd heard in his rant was that he was hurting and had been for a long time. He didn't have a Farley to protect and guide him. He'd been beaten down so many times he'd learned to strike first and strike hard. It was how he survived. I couldn't hate a man for that.

When I found him, he was in the lavatory preparing to down the pills our handlers had instructed us to take. They were meant to keep us more alert and able to go for long periods of time without sleep. We'd lost more than one man to the madness that was a side-effect of prolonged usage. Which was why most of us had silently agreed to flush whatever medications the program gave us down the toilets. I'd assumed he was also off the pills and was saddened that I missed the signs.

Few in the unit would have dared corner Ray the way I

did that day. He pushed to get past me, but I blocked his way out. "You need to stop taking those," I said with my arms folded across my chest.

"Mind your own fucking business," he growled.

"Your business *is* my business," I answered calmly. "We're in this together."

His laugh was cold. "That's what they want us to believe, but what happens when one of us steps out of line? They're gone. Taken in the night. Do we look for them? Say their name afterward? Or do we just go on like the good little soldiers they want us to be and do as we're told?"

His question rocked me back onto my heels. The losses to our unit had been substantial both by death and removal. "We need to stay focused, Ray."

With a curl of his lip, he asked, "How much thought will you give me if they come for me tonight because I stepped out of line? Will you have my back then or will you do nothing and let them take me?" When I didn't have an immediate answer, his fists clenched at his side. "So, get out of my way, and let's not pretend we give a shit about each other."

I didn't move, partly because he was going to kill himself by continuing to take those pills but mostly because he was right. Since joining the program we'd been told to keep our eyes on the prize and the missions. Nothing else mattered, nothing else could. We were instructed to not ask questions. But we should have. "If they come for you tonight, I'll get you away from them or die at your side trying."

He frowned. "Sure. I believe that."

"You have my word."

Eyes narrowed, he spat. "Promises mean nothing."

I held his gaze. "They do when they come from me. You're not in this alone, Ray. Not unless you want to be. But trust goes both ways. Throw those pills in the toilet."

He looked down at the bottle in his hand. "I've been on them too long. You've seen what happens when people try to stop."

I had. Some had psychotic breaks and were taken away. "We'll hide whatever side effects you have."

"We?"

"All of us. Together. Because you're a damn good soldier and the war needs you. *We* need you. You'll never be able to save the world unless you start seeing yourself as one of us."

He threw out the pills and we weathered that storm together. And no one came for him. Maybe they knew. Maybe they didn't. Either way, we would have fought for him. What he did to Hugh, as well as what I told everyone afterward, changed the unit, even though neither was spoken of after that day.

We'd become family.

Where is my unit now?

Am I the only one left?

Did what happened to me happen to them? Or did they go on to live post-war lives?

My last memory is asking Hugh to pass a punch down to Ray. Ray apologized later, but his apology hadn't sounded related to what he'd said about me.

Then there was a flash.

Then nothing.

Now this . . . prison.

There's a vibration of a voice. It's her. I don't know what she's saying, but she's near.

I call out to her. There's no response because I'm incapable of sound.

I don't want to want her . . . to feel this desperation for her presence. During much of my life I've been closed off from the world, but never have I felt this overwhelming need for someone.

She wraps herself around me and I'm no longer cold. I'm held, caressed and so turned on the past ceases to matter. She's all there is and all I crave.

Chapter Nine

Cheryl

Providence, Rhode Island
2024

W HEN I RETURN to my apartment, I pick up the spoon from the shelf I placed it on earlier that day and sigh. It's embarrassing to admit how often I think about it. I don't allow myself to, but I want to keep it with me—always.

I've told myself to return it, but I don't want to. I've picked it up with the intention of putting it in a mailer and sending it to Mercedes, but something happens each time I touch it.

It's exciting—like I'm touching something forbidden.

But it's more than that.

The spoon warms to my touch, welcomes me, feels more mine than anything I've ever owned. When I put it down and force myself to walk away from it, I ache a little as if I'm leaving a piece of myself behind.

Sometimes I stand there, looking at it, like I've been called to it.

A spoon. A fucking spoon.

The back of the handle says it's .925 silver and the name of the company who made it. Nothing else.

I looked it over with a magnifying glass. Guess what I saw? Silver with a deep scratch. I don't know what else I expected to see, but it wasn't there. I'd love to take it to Ashley's lab and get it under a microscope, but I'm not ready to answer more questions about it.

I'm a single woman in my prime. I have a little fun now and then, but nothing too wild. I can still count the number of men I have been with on one hand. Well, if I had more fingers I could, but I don't count the boyfriend I slept with in high school. Neither of us knew what we were doing.

I should have known it wouldn't be good when he told me he didn't want me to see him naked. I was a virgin so I wasn't exactly an expert on sex, but I was pretty certain we weren't supposed to stay clothed.

If you're curious, it's possible. You can get a lot done if you're creative about how you move the layers aside. I went along with it because I thought I loved him. Funny what a woman will do when she thinks that.

We didn't last and when it ended I was heartbroken. Looking back, I see our breakup as the best thing he ever did for me. I'd confused liking to be with someone with liking to be with him.

If someone offered me a chance to go back and do high school over, I wouldn't. I struggled back then, even more than I struggle now. I still worry too much about what others think of me, but I'm kinder to myself when I catch myself doing it. Perfection isn't attainable and I'm learning to accept that I'll always be a work in progress.

Ashley's end-of-meal advice was that I should just do it—the spoon. She thinks after I prove to myself that the spoon is nothing more than a piece of metal, I'll be able to stop using it as an excuse to avoid talking to my parents.

I turn the spoon in my hand. Is Ashley right? That would explain why I feel drawn to it—it represents freedom from the pressure of making a decision my parents will think is wrong.

Being wrong isn't as bad as being indecisive, right?

I caress the neck of the spoon with my thumb. What would be the difference between using this or my vibrator? And no one would need to know.

My heart races as I walk into my bedroom with the spoon. Am I actually going to do this?

I place the spoon on my bed, just below my pillow.

Not taking my eyes off the spoon, I step out of my shoes and socks. This is insane, but it's also fucking exciting. They say sex happens first in a woman's mind, and right now I believe it. There's nothing enticing about touching a spoon, but the fantasy of a beefy man appearing in my bedroom— well, that's the turn on.

Nothing will appear because spoons don't become men.

But that doesn't stop me from sliding out of my under-clothes. The chill in the air makes it tempting to leave my shirt on, but when I imagine a super soldier appearing between my legs, I don't imagine being partially dressed.

Naked, I pick up the spoon and slide beneath my com-forter.

Let's do this.

Am I supposed to kiss it? I hold it up to my lips. The heat of my breath fogs the back of its bowl. Now what?

I'm not freaking making out with a spoon.

Closing my eyes, I run the back of it down the side of my neck. Um, yes. That's actually not bad. Sliding it beneath the comforter, I use it to circle one nipple, loving the way the metal heats against my skin. Slowly, I move it to my other breast and suck in a breath as I swear it begins to move against me. I imagine the metal is a tongue and a talented one at that.

I brush it between my breasts, making erotic circles as I move it lower . . . and lower . . . and lower until . . . ah, yes. I part my legs wider and use the back of its bowl against my clit. Slow and gentle at first. Lightly. In my mind the spoon is the experienced thumb of a man who wants this to be the beginning of forever with me.

In true super soldier form, he wants my pleasure to come before his.

I increase the speed a little, imagining him growling

naughty suggestions into my ear. Just when I begin to think I'd rather finish with a toy than a utensil, the spoon begins to vibrate.

Vibrate.

At first I think I'm imagining it, but as I hold it against me, I don't care if the movement is coming from it or my wrist. It's perfection and I'm so close to coming.

So close.

Heat begins to unfurl in my stomach.

Just a little bit more.

Yes.

Just like that.

Oh, my God.

I'm going to—

A heavy weight descends on me, smothering the air out of my lungs. Metal digs into my bare chest and a chin bangs into my forehead.

A deep, masculine voice says, "What the hell just happened?"

I'd tell him, but I can't breathe.

Plus, I'm struggling to believe what my senses tell me. I'm being crushed by a huge man in a military uniform. God, he smells good. Even if this kills me, what a way to go.

As if realizing he has a person beneath him, he raises himself onto his elbows and looks down into my eyes. "Who are you?" He glances around. "How did I get here?"

If he doesn't know, there's no way I'm going to tell him

what I was doing. Instead I bring my hands up between us to touch his broad chest, grazing the medals there.

He looks down and sees my bare breasts. His nostrils flare, his eyes widen, and his face turns bright red. "You're naked."

I nod.

"I've never actually seen . . ." He stops, shakes his head and brings his gaze up to meet mine again. "Who are you?"

"My name is Cheryl Briggs."

"Where are we?"

I know the answer to that, but it's impossible to form a coherent thought when the bulge of him is pressed against my thigh. I swallow hard.

If this is real, then it would make sense that he has questions.

Focus.

What would you want to know if you reappeared eighty years in the future?

"We're in my apartment. The year is twenty twenty-four. You were accidentally turned into silverware and I just freed you from that."

He frowns, cocks his head to the side and looks around as he absorbs the news. He's deliciously tense, every rock-hard inch of him. If I was asked to design a fantasy sex partner, he checked all the boxes. Big. Strong. Square jaw. Dark hair, cut short, but with enough length that some flopped over onto his forehead. And those eyes . . . I've never seen any like them. They're two-toned, with white flecks in them. Gorgeous. I could spend a lifetime staring into them.

I tell myself he needs information and compassion more than he needs me to start humping his leg, but I'm fighting the urge to tear his clothing off and have a question-answer session later.

I should be scared.

Things like this don't happen.

It's possible there was a drug on the spoon, and this is just a wild trip. I was drugged recently, though, and it was nothing like this.

He's real. At least, I'm nearly positive he is. Curiosity trumps sanity and my hand goes to his bulge. It's hard. My God, it's huge, just like the rest of him. I bite my bottom lip and check his expression.

He's breathing raggedly, but his eyes darken with emotion. I reluctantly drop my hand to one side. "Twenty twenty-four? Eighty years? I've been gone *eighty* years?"

I nod. "Is your name Jack Sully?" It has to be.

Instead of answering my question, he asks, "Everyone I love is gone, aren't they?"

Well, this is a mood killer. "Probably? Yes."

"My friends. My mother. Farley."

What could I say to that? Nothing. I hadn't expected summoning a super soldier of my own would be so sad.

"I promised I'd go back to them. I gave them my word." His voice is raw. "They died not knowing what happened to me. Probably waiting for me to return."

"I'm sorry."

And . . . poof . . . just like that he's gone.

What the fuck?

I throw the comforter back and there between my thighs is the damn spoon.

After retrieving it, I sit up, spin, and lower my feet to the floor.

Okay.

Okay.

Okay.

I did not just imagine that.

I stand and pace the room. Hugh changed into a fork right in front of me to prove to me that he was a fork. Jack . . . if that even was Jack . . . was obviously in shock and changed back because of it.

What do I do now?

Do I call Mercedes and tell her that I believe her?

Ask her for advice?

Tell her it worked?

She'll probably rush over and ask me to bring him back.

Then what? I bring him back while they wait?

Talk about pressure.

What if I can't? What if that was a one-and-done?

Still naked, I walk through my apartment, spoon in hand, mumbling to myself. "Whatever was done to the soldiers seems to reverse in response to the chemicals released in the male body during arousal. Or pheromones. I need to look at this like an experiment and not an erotic dream. The first stimulus resulted in Jack appearing. Emotional distress resulted in him reverting back to a spoon. Replicating the process as exactly as I can is the only way to test that theory.

I hesitate at the door of my bedroom.

This feels crazy.

But I didn't imagine Jack being here.

And I do want him back.

My phone buzzes with a message.

I check it quickly. It's Greg. He wants to know if I want to go to dinner.

I answer that I can't because I have plans, then toss my phone to the side and look down at the spoon in my hand.

Plans. That's one way to describe what I'm about to do.

I have to know.

Okay, here we go.

I ease myself back on the bed and cover myself with the comforter again. What did I do first? I blew on the spoon.

I bring the spoon to the front of my lips and blow on it.

Nothing happens, but nothing happened the first time.

I shiver as I run the spoon down my neck. It was exciting the first time, there's a whole new level of anticipation now that I know this ends with a man actually appearing.

Nothing yet.

My hand is shaking as I use the spoon to circle my nipples again. First one, then the other. Now that I've seen his lips, it's even easier to imagine them on me instead of the spoon. This time as I make slow circles down my stomach, my sex is already throbbing.

I part my legs and place the back of the spoon's bowl on my clit. This was what I was doing when he appeared. I begin to move the spoon, slowly, deliberately . . . not realizing I'm holding my breath until I get lightheaded and gasp for air.

The spoon remains motionless and I fight back disappointment. I'm too far in to stop now. I press the spoon harder against my clit and begin to move it back and forth faster and faster.

I'm alone, but my body doesn't care. It heats and readies for pleasure. Just when I think I may have to bring myself to completion, the spoon begins to move and my hand tightens around it.

Oh, yes.

A little jackhammer on my nub.

Perfect.

So good.

I squirm beneath it; one of my hands grips the sheet at my side while the other holds him in place. I close my eyes and imagine Jack is on me, pounding into me as I cry out his name and beg him not to stop. Heat spreads through me and I give myself over to it.

Just as I do, my hand is stretched wide and the spoon turns once again into a fully dressed Jack. This time, as the air is crushed out of me, I'm riding out an orgasm, and the shock of it pushes my pleasure to a whole new level. I both die and am reborn in that moment—it's that fucking good.

I'm still coming down from heaven when Jack pushes himself up onto his elbows to lessen his weight on me. I almost tell him not to, but I do need oxygen.

We are not at all on the same emotional page. His eyes are tormented and I'm still shuddering from the orgasm.

"What just happened?" he demands.

I'm not ready to share that.

He looks down at my bare breasts again. I know this can't be easy for him, but I can't deny enjoying how his nostrils flare again and his cock hardens against my leg.

Breathlessly, I'm determined to do this better. "Jack?"

He nods. "Yes. Sorry, I don't know where I went or how."

Breathe. He needs answers. "From what I understand about this, you and your unit were changed into silverware at an award ceremony. Your physical state must somehow be linked to your mental one because when you thought about the people in your past you became a spoon again."

"A spoon? I don't understand."

Yeah, it doesn't really make sense to me, either. "Try not to go anywhere and I'll get you the answers you need."

He glances at my breasts again, flushes, meets my gaze, and asks, "Why are we in bed together?"

Oh, God. I have to tell him. "It's the only way to bring

you back."

"What's the only way?"

I swallow hard. "Being intimate with you."

He frowns. "While I'm a spoon?"

He doesn't believe me.

Or he doesn't want to imagine that scene.

I don't either.

This is not a conversation I ever imagined I'd have. "Yes."

He rolls off me and I feel lost without his touch. He's looking at me like we're strangers and that completely makes sense since we are. "You're the woman I've sensed around me? Touching me? Washing me?"

I pull the comforter up to cover myself. Putting it like that sounds bad. "That's me. I was told I might be able to help free you, but I didn't believe it until now."

He looks around the room and then down at himself beneath the comforter. "The award ceremony. We were celebrating winning the war against Germany." His eyes rivet to mine. "Did we win the whole war?"

"We did."

"How? When?"

I've done enough research into the story Mercedes told me about these soldiers that I know the timeline. "Months after you disappeared, we dropped two atomic bombs on Japan, and that ended the war."

His expression fills with horror. "The United States did

that? *We* made the atomic bomb and used it? Against a military base?" He goes pale. "Or civilians?"

Just above a whisper, I say, "We dropped it on Hiroshima and Nagasaki."

"No!" His head is shaking violently back and forth. "We made sure that bomb would never be created. We gathered the scientists. We . . ." I watch helplessly as he processes the role he played in the horrific ending to the war, and he goes quiet and motionless for a moment. "We gave our country what they said the world needed to be protected from and they *used* it." His breathing becomes ragged. "We didn't save anyone."

Oh, no.

I know that look.

I reach for him, but poof, he's gone.

Fuck.

A few minutes later, I'm dressed again. The spoon is in the kitchen in the sink like a spoon should be.

I need help.

I call Mercedes. She answers breathlessly, and I wonder if she and Hugh were doing what I did. Nothing I say will sound normal or logical so I don't even try to make it. "He was here, Mercedes. I brought Jack back."

"She brought Jack back," Mercedes exclaims.

In the background, I hear Hugh say, "Thank God. Put him on the phone."

"I can't," I say slowly.

"You didn't let him leave, did you?" Mercedes asks in a rush. "He shouldn't be out there alone before we acclimate him to this time period."

I clear my throat and glance at the spoon "He's right here, but he's a spoon again."

"Oh," Mercedes says. "He's a spoon again, Hugh."

A moment later, she says, "Have you tried bringing him back? Just do whatever you did the first time."

"I tried that. He came back and left again."

"I don't understand."

I share what Jack said each time before he disappeared.

The next voice on the phone is Hugh's. "I should have anticipated this. Jack was close to his family. I need to talk to him. We have clothes in his size for him. We'll bring them over. While we're there, get him to come back and I'll make sure he stays this time."

"Um, no. I can't . . . not with you here."

"We'll bring ice cream. All you have to do is use him to eat something you enjoy and think about how much you want him to return."

My breath rushes out of me. "Wait, hold on, all I had to do was use him to eat ice cream and that would have brought him back?"

In the background, Mercedes says, "Oh, yeah, I forgot that worked the first time with us. Are you saying we could just do it that way, Hugh?"

Hugh sounds like a man choking on a guilty laugh.

"Seriously?" Mercedes jokes. "Tonight you're sleeping in the kitchen."

I bury my face in my hand. "No sex necessary. Well, that would have been good information to share about an hour ago."

It's Mercedes' turn to let out a guilty laugh. "I'm sorry. I should have remembered it can also be that easy. If it helps, though, Hugh says he can feel everything I do to him while he's a fork. So Jack must too. And if you brought him back that means he liked it."

I sure hope so because I don't know how to ask a utensil for consent.

"We'll be right over," Mercedes promises. "And I'll bring ice cream."

"Fine," I say while dueling with a tsunami of emotions. I'm embarrassed, confused about how any of this can be real, and oddly excited to see Jack again.

After I end the call, I walk over to Jack and pick him up. If he can really feel everything I do to the spoon, he knows I'm holding him now. My cheeks warm as I think about how many times I've washed him off when he wasn't even dirty. How had that felt to him?

Will he make me feel that good when he returns?

A little voice in my head suggests that I'm being selfish by focusing on how I feel. I'm not the one who woke up eighty years in the future. He didn't ask for any of this and might not want anything to do with me.

For all I know he might have been in love with someone he left behind. Or his preference might be for someone who doesn't have a vagina.

I lean against the sink, and as I look at the spoon, I'm convinced I see a shadow of Jack in the reflection of it. I'm thoroughly embarrassed, but I put how I feel aside and try to imagine how overwhelming this must be for him. Although I have issues with my parents, I'd be devastated if they were suddenly gone . . . along with everyone else I know and care about.

I might choose being trapped in cutlery over that. "I'm sorry. I didn't think about how hard this might be for you. I'll do better."

I pour a little soap over him and give him a good scrub. "Sorry, about this, but if I'm going to be eating off you . . ."

The spoon doesn't move. I probably deserve the cold shoulder he's giving me. The whole idea of a lusty super soldier being trapped in silverware and appearing like my own personal sexual genie, ready and willing to be mine is the stuff porn is made of. Actually, porn usually has less of a plot, but you know what I mean.

This isn't a game. There's a real man in that spoon, and he's hurting.

After drying him off, I hug him to my chest. "We can be friends, Jack. Don't choose oblivion over being here. We'll help you."

Chapter Ten

Jack

Providence, Rhode Island
2024

I DON'T KNOW what's real and what's not anymore. Nor do I understand how I keep returning to this place where I'm neither dead nor alive.

Twice, I experienced an overwhelming pull and went to her—Cheryl. She has a name now. And a face. A beautiful, perfect face with intense dark eyes and a body that fit perfectly beneath mine. Had I not been reeling from the shock of becoming myself again, I would have sampled those plump lips of hers and drank her in.

Although I had sex and knew the feel of the female form intimately, I've never experienced the pleasure visually. God, she was stunning . . . at least what little of her I allowed myself to soak in.

She's still with me. Washing me again. I feel her all

around me and the temptation to return to her is strong but I don't know how to.

Is the ache in my heart what holds me back? Eighty years. I left everyone and everything I cared about behind . . . for what? If what Cheryl said is true, the goal of Project Inkwell was a lie. We didn't save the world from the horror of a weapon of mass destruction, we stole that weapon for our side and used it.

The weight of that rests on my shoulders.

I have to live with that.

If I'm even still alive.

I think back to my last moments in 1945. We were being fed a fancy meal and receiving medals of honor. That wasn't how we wanted to celebrate, though. Our thoughts were on how we'd slip away after the dinner and seek female companionship.

For a variety of reasons, it had been years since any of us had allowed ourselves to think about anything beyond the mission. We were told the fate of the world was in the balance. That day, Germany's surrender was the sign we'd been waiting for. We could finally take a break from saving the world and indulge in a little carnal pleasure.

Carefully.

Since our transformation, none of us knew if we were still safe for anyone to have sex with. We not only had increased strength and stamina, but parts of our bodies could expand and stretch. Enough of us had accidentally killed non-unit adversaries before we learned to control the power in our moves. No one wanted to hurt an innocent in what should be a mutually satisfying experience.

We weren't alone in craving to connect with another human that day. The announcement of the end of the war had many people putting aside their inhibitions and brazenly celebrating with strangers. At least, that's what we'd heard and none of us wanted to miss out on that opportunity.

The irony of what Cheryl said was necessary to bring me back wasn't lost on me. We died craving sex, of course that would have the power to reverse whatever happened to us. The universe sure had a twisted sense of humor.

I'm not complaining. Nature always finds a way, and usually it's at the most elemental level. Fucked up as this all is, this time it almost makes sense.

The warmth of her touch is replaced by a jolt of cold. What is she doing now? The past and my desire to make sense of it is pushed aside and replaced by the sensation of being surrounded by her. Cold on the top, but hot and wet everywhere else.

I'm in her mouth.

As a spoon.

Her tongue laps the back of me, her lips close around me. I can taste her and the experience shakes me to the core. I don't just want more of her, I need it. All of me wants to belong to her, and I want to claim her for my own.

I'm aching for her.

Then shaking for her.

No, she pulls me from her mouth and I'm devastated by the loss of our connection.

I can't think.

I can't stay.

I have to be with her.

With a jolt I am myself again, only this time I hit the floor with a thud on a rug rather than the sweet softness of Cheryl. When I stand, she's what I seek. She's, disappointingly, fully dressed, but she's there and even more beautiful than I remember.

"I'm back," I say hoarsely.

"You are." Her voice is breathless and filled with wonder.

"Jack," a familiar voice booms and tears my attention from her.

I let out a relief-filled laugh. "Hugh." Damned if his eyes aren't shining like he's about to cry.

He steps closer. "I realize this is all a shock, but you need to stay. Freeing the rest of our unit is our mission now. We'll deal with how we feel about the past and all the shit that happened back then later. Right now, focus on the good we can do and the people who need us."

"Understood." I stand straighter as his words activate the part of me that chose going to war over the safety of my home in Rhode Island. I never hesitated to follow Hugh's commands or take his side in any battle because he's a man of integrity. In all the years we fought side by side, he kept the welfare of our country and our unit his priority.

Like me, he'd been misled and was likely carrying a good amount of guilt for what we'd done, but feelings came second to duty. Our unit was our second family . . . our only family now.

"Where is our unit?"

"Trapped in silverware the way we were. At least, I think so."

"Trapped in silverware." I echo his words as I struggle to make them not sound impossible. "How? Who did this?"

"I don't have an answer to either of those questions—not yet. You and I have a lot we need to figure out, but now that we've brought you back I'm optimistic that we can bring back the others."

My attention returns to Cheryl who flashes me a shy smile. Duty over feelings. "Thank you for . . ."

She blushes and looks away. "You're welcome."

She is so damn beautiful, and I feel as drawn to her now as I did earlier. If we didn't have an audience I'd tell her there's no reason to be embarrassed, but the conversation I'd like to have with her is one we should have alone. I turn back to Hugh and, this time, notice he has a petite brunette at his side.

He puts an arm around her. "Jack Sully, this is my fiancée, Mercedes Hopper."

"Your fiancée? How long have you been back?"

The protective way his arm shifts her closer tells me more

about their relationship than his expression does. "Long enough to know."

I nod once. Understood. "Is it truly twenty twenty-four?"

"It is." There's no longing in Hugh's voice, no sadness. Nothing that reflects how I feel, knowing the option of going home is no longer there.

He seems to sense where my thoughts have gone. "Jack. We knew the risks when we joined. We're lucky to still be here."

"Lucky." That wasn't the word I would have chosen to describe waking up eighty years in the future. He was correct, though. Not one of us had been guaranteed a trip home. War is an ugly thing and maybe surviving it, regardless of the situation one finds themselves in afterward, is something to be grateful for. Gratitude wasn't possible yet, but maybe it would come. "What do you need me to do?"

Hugh holds my gaze and the expression in his eyes reminds me of the night I'd repeated Ray's questions to him. I'd asked him then if he would stand with me against Falcon and our handlers if they came for any of the rest of us. Like me, he believed in our missions and that we were saving the world. Would he throw away something that important for one man? A man who might have earned being taken away? Where did his loyalty lie? Where should it? He didn't have the answers then.

He doesn't have the answers to my questions now.

Mercedes pipes in. "Thankfully, Hugh and I were where

you and Cheryl are so you won't have to go through all the: Is he real? How does this work? We've even created your new identity."

I glance at Cheryl. She's looking a little shell-shocked. "You okay?"

She gives me a head-to-toe-and-back-up perusal before saying, "I think so. How are you handling this? It must be confusing."

"It's definitely that, but I've been in worse situations." That's true. When we first started taking the injections, many of the men we'd signed on with started dying . . . that was bad. I waited, understanding I might be next, and preparing myself mentally in case I was. I survived that trial by fire. I'll survive this.

She clears her throat and leans toward me. "I don't want you to think you owe me anything for bringing you back. It's obviously a chemical process, possibly a reaction to female pheromones. Because of that, there's a high probability that intimacy with any woman would produce the same effect."

Part of me respects her bold honesty. It reveals an integrity I'm relieved to see is still part of society. Still, her words gut me, because it's inconceivable that the connection I feel to her isn't reciprocal. If it's not, though, I need to be as respectful. "I appreciate that. Thank you."

Mercedes' voice rises an octave. "Hugh, do you think that's true? Any woman could change you back?"

He hugs her to him and kisses her forehead. "We'll never know because I'll never test that theory."

She melts against him and I inhale sharply. Could any woman make me feel the way Cheryl does? I've never felt this connected to anyone before. Then again, I've never been a spoon either. I don't know what to think.

She brought me back ... three times. That's already more than I could ever repay someone for. She also made sure Hugh was here for me this time, and she's more worried about how I feel than how she does.

The temptation to kiss her and tell her everything will be okay is nearly as strong as my desire to return to her was. No, I couldn't feel this for someone else. She's smart, though, to question the process and not blindly trust in a happily ever after.

The world is a twisted place that doesn't play by a predictable set of rules. I need time to figure out what the hell happened to me and who I am as a result of it. And she obviously needs time to get to know me.

Cheryl and I exchange a long, awkward look before I tear my gaze away.

She says, "You should probably get out of that uniform." Her face turns bright red when that snaps my attention back to her. "And into the clothes Hugh brought. Can't have any naked super soldiers running around." She presses her lips together and looks so uncomfortable I grab the clothes from Hugh and hold back a smile. *She wants me naked.*

You first, doll. And soon. I need to see the rest of you.

"Where should I change?" I can't help teasing her just a little. "The bedroom?" If she didn't look mortified, I would joke about knowing that room well.

"Sure." She points toward a door. "It's over there."

Damned if it isn't difficult to walk away from her. I stand there, frowning, because I don't know a single thing about her, but I want to know everything. I want to see that worry line leave her forehead and laughter replace the shadow in her eyes.

After another intense, silent exchange, she says, "Are you hungry? I'm sure you'll want to leave with Hugh, but I could make a snack for everyone first."

I walk over to her, bend down and whisper in her ear. "Do you want me to leave?"

Her breath fans my neck as she answers huskily, "I want you to do what you want to do."

Does she? Really? I brush my lips over the shell of her ear. "Even if that's kiss you?" She gasps, and this time, I smile. I don't want to rush her, but I also need to know if she's feeling any of what I am. "Cheryl?"

"Yes?" That one breathless word tells me everything I need to know.

"I'm not going anywhere this time."

Chapter Eleven

Cheryl

Providence, Rhode Island
2024

"HE LIKES YOU," Mercedes announces from within the circle of Hugh's arms.

I meet her fiancé's eyes. "Does he have a choice?"

Hugh shrugs. "I don't know."

It wasn't the answer I was hoping for. Yes, Jack is everything Mercedes said he would be—big, kind-hearted, and something she'd left out—gorgeous. But if the only reason he likes me is because I freed him . . . I don't want that.

Mercedes looks up at Hugh. "Do you feel like *you* don't have a choice?"

There's so much emotion in his eyes that my throat clogs up. "I found my other half when we met. You understand me in a way no one else ever has. We would have chosen each other no matter how we met. That's how I feel."

She hugs him tightly before answering. "And you're the answer to the questions I never thought my heart would ask."

"Hey, that's my line." He chuckles at that and kisses her.

Okay, so what they have is real, but even a broken clock is right twice a day. Unable to be in their bubble of love a moment longer, I walk a few feet away and sink onto my couch. They need a moment alone and I need to think.

I diddled a spoon and now I have a World War II super soldier changing in my bedroom. That's fine. Completely normal. Just like any other day.

He said he's not leaving this time like there's an option for him to stay with me. Where? Here in my apartment? On my couch? In my bed?

He's already been in my bed. If I'm completely honest with myself, I've already orgasmed with him on top of me, so . . .

Oh, my God. If things work out with him, I'll never be able to look anyone in the eye when they ask me how we met. Nope, our entire relationship . . . friendship . . . spoonship . . . whatever the fuck this is will be based on the lie I invent so people don't think about me what I thought about Mercedes when she first told me Hugh was a fork.

I shouldn't have judged her as harshly as I did. I remember all the times I felt unheard and dismissed by my parents. It bothers me that I may have made Mercedes feel the same way.

An apology is due, but right now there are more pressing matters.

Hugh and Mercedes appear happy, but have they considered how much danger they could be in? If Hugh and Jack were part of a government experiment, I bet what happened at that award dinner was deliberate. Someone tried to end the project—permanently. The US? A foreign country?

Eighty years is long enough for an individual threat to die off—but a government? No, they have long memories and enduring agendas.

My friends and I hadn't been careful while researching Project Inkwell. None of us thought there was a reason to be. World War II happened so long ago. I need to tell my friends to stop looking into it until we know who we're dealing with.

They'll have questions.

What can I tell them? In every movie, when someone reaches out to a friend with something like this, it always ends with a betrayal that puts everyone at risk.

Until now my greatest concerns have been internal. Which job should I take? Who do I want to please? What makes me happy?

Now I need to know who I can trust.

I have a circle of friends I really enjoy, but how well do I really know them? We met in various college study groups. We've shared being drunk, sober, stressed, confused, inspired, entertained . . . but how would any of them respond to danger? I have no idea.

I'd like to think Ashley and I are tight and would protect each other, but potentially getting messed up with some government cover-up isn't at all like backing down a sneering stranger.

Nothing Mercedes told me about the work Project Inkwell did during the war had shocked me. Handing German scientists and their families over to the United States was just another war detail for the history books—until I saw the horror in Jack's eyes when he learned what the result of that action had been.

Now I don't know what to do . . . or if there is anyone I can turn to for advice. What will the government do if they find out Jack and his unit didn't die?

I'm right back to feeling alone and scared and I hate it.

I don't want this secret. This responsibility.

I'm no hero.

I'm just a woman trying to be strong and brave in a world full of things I have no idea how to battle.

"Are you hyperventilating?" Mercedes asks as she joins me on the couch. "Because you look like you might pass out.

"I've never even held a gun," I announce.

"Okay."

My stomach churns nervously. "You should have asked someone else to bring Jack back."

Hugh comes to stand before us. His expression is difficult to read. "Jack needs you to be strong, Cheryl. We all do.

I don't know where your head is at or what you're afraid of, but the lives of a dozen men depend on you holding your shit together."

"That's not fair, Hugh. And it's too much pressure to put on her," Mercedes says gently.

Hugh's expression tightens. "Out of everyone in the unit, Jack is the one I trust the most. He's also about a hundred times stronger than I am. We don't know what will happen as we try to wake the others, but with him at my side, I'm confident any situation can be handled."

Mercedes stands and takes one of Hugh's hands in both of hers. "I thought you were excited to bring your friends back."

"Not excited." He pulls her to him and tucks her beneath his chin. Over her head, our gazes lock. "Determined. No one gets left behind. We stand and win or fall and die together. When we promised that to each other, we went from a unit of soldiers to brothers."

I clasp my hands together on my lap. "But?"

"We don't all share the same definition of duty and honor."

My mouth rounds. "Oh."

That's not good.

He continues, "The men followed me because they trusted me to know how to handle situations. They trusted Jack because he could not only get us out alive but also kept us from turning on each other. He's a good man and an unmatched soldier. He can't go back. You need to help us keep him here."

Fear shoots through me. Are these men war heroes, criminals, or somewhere in between? Had someone thought they were too dangerous to return to freedom after the war? Were they? "What are you asking me to do?"

"Don't confuse him more than he already is." He glances at the woman in his arms. "Mercedes has been my rock. When nothing else made sense, we did. Jack will see you the same way. Don't take that from him."

I slowly shake my head. "He deserves to know he might have options."

"It's not for you to decide what any of us do or don't deserve. Jack will need someone to show him how to navigate this time period. We need someone we can trust. Is that you or isn't it?"

Hugh's question hangs in the air.

Jack's voice is deep and calm. "That's enough, Hugh. Cheryl doesn't owe us anything."

I shoot to my feet and turn to face Jack. The way he's looking at me, like he's prepared to defend me against even his friend, has me weak in the knees.

Behind me, Mercedes says, "He's right, Hugh. I know how much is at stake, but they may or may not have what we do. You can't order them to fall in love."

Jack was strikingly impressive in his uniform, but the blue cotton T-shirt is stretched over his bulging muscles in the most sinfully decadent way. My gaze dips lower and my breath catches in my throat as I soak in his powerful thighs and the prominent bulge between them. All that can be mine . . .

Without taking his eyes off me, Jack asks, "Hugh, do we have a way to stay in touch?"

"Yes. We bought you a portable phone. My number is in there. Do you want me to show you how to use it?"

"That won't be necessary."

"Okay." Hugh referenced a bag placed near the door. "We had IDs made for you. Your name is now Jack Mendon. Your phone is in that bag. A wallet too. In the wallet, you'll find your IDs, paper money, as well as a plastic card that you can use to pay for things. I put five hundred dollars on the account."

Jack's eyes widen for just an instant. "That's a lot of money."

"Not anymore. You sure you don't want me to stick around and explain a few things to you?"

"No, Cheryl will teach me."

I'm a modern woman who would normally protest that Jack should ask me first if that's something I want to do, but the firmness of his tone is turning me on.

While pinning me in place with those amazing eyes of his, Jack says, "She and I have some things to talk out. I'll contact you when the situation here is settled."

"Settled?" I echo just above whisper. What did that

mean?

Mercedes rushes over to me and gives my side a hug. "Call me if you need anything."

It's sweet, and I thank her, but I can't pull my gaze from Jack's.

There's the sound of my apartment door opening and closing as Hugh and Mercedes leave and we're alone.

I don't know about Jack, but I'm finding it difficult to breathe. My heart is thudding wildly in my chest. My hands are cold and shaking. If there wasn't a couch between us, would I already be in his arms?

The urge to be there is strong, but so is my need to understand the situation before I dive into it.

"What do you want to do?"

I let out a shaky breath and swallow hard. "In regards to what?"

"Us."

I sway on my feet. "Is there an us? We just met."

He leans forward, bringing his eyes level to mine, and braces himself with two hands on the couch. "It doesn't feel that way."

Oh, boy. "I try not to have sex with men I hardly know."

His eyebrows rise then humor fills his expression. "That's a healthy goal. Is it a difficult one for you?"

Bringing both hands to my face, I hide for a moment then remind myself that I don't owe him any explanations. "I'm not a virgin if that's what you're asking."

"Nor am I." His lips curl in a smile and I don't like that he might have taken my admission as a green light to having sex.

Despite the lack of judgment in his eyes, I feel compelled to say, "Public opinion of chastity has changed since your time."

"I see." Some of his amusement fades. "How about monogamy? Has that lost value as well?"

"I guess it depends on who you ask."

"The only opinion I care about on that matter is yours."

"Oh, then, yes, it's still important."

"Good." He searches my face. "Do you currently have a man in your life?"

I shake my head.

"Do you want one?"

I open my mouth to answer, but no words come out. Do I want just any man? No. Do I want this one? It frightens me how easy it would be to say yes.

Yes to helping him.

Yes to fucking him.

Yes to putting my life and my friends at risk for him.

I clear my throat and fight to remain logical about this. "I don't know."

"That's fair." After a moment, he nods and straightens. "I like you. You seem like a good person. I realize, though, this is a lot for anyone to take in. If you want me to, I'll call Hugh and tell him to come back for me."

The thought of him leaving fills me with a sudden and inexplicable sadness. I should let him go before I'm pulled deeper into what might be a messy and dangerous situation. "Stay." The word is out while I'm still debating if he should.

His smile starts in his eyes and then goes to his lips. "Okay."

"Okay," I whisper back.

"I feel connected to you, Cheryl, in a way I haven't felt for another woman. I've tasted you, craved you, given myself over to the pull of you. Has it been the same for you?"

I want to tell him it has. I don't know what stops me from sharing that since the moment I touched him I felt he was mine.

His expression softens. "Too much too soon. I understand. We don't have to rush. Let's get to know each other. I have no idea how the world has changed or what I'll need to learn to fit in. I sure could use a friend to help me with that."

A friend.

Could I be that? It probably requires forgetting how good it felt to be naked and pinned down by him.

"You'll sleep on the couch." The words burst out of me. I groan. What am I—twelve?

And it's not even what I want, but it's what I *should* want.

"After I bend you over it?"

God, yes. Well, at least this isn't easy for him either. My mouth drops open and he lets out a hearty laugh.

"Too soon?"

I stand there, frozen, feeling like a virgin on her wedding night. What's wrong with me? "Sorry. I'm nervous."

He nods. "How do we change that?"

I'm not used to someone being so direct and . . . wholesome? He did suggest he'd like to bend me over the couch, but in a quiet, playful way. Despite his size, I feel safe with him. Protected. "Want to go for a drive?" I need to get out of my apartment.

"In a car?"

I laugh. "Yes, in a car. It'll be easier to show you how things have changed than tell you."

"I appreciate that. Thank you." His tone is so sincere that I'm reminded of how vulnerable he must feel. He looks a hell of a lot calmer than I would in his situation.

I dig out the phone and wallet Hugh left for him and walk around the couch to hand them to Jack. "Take them with you. When we find a spot to stop, I'll show you how the phone works."

After Jack pockets them, he closes a hand over one of mine. My hand shakes beneath his touch. He frowns. "Are you afraid of me?"

"No." My face warms. I can't begin to unravel how he makes me feel. So, I simply repeat myself huskily. "No."

One of his hands cups the side of my face and he dips down until his lips gently brush over mine. Heat sears through me and in that moment, no one could convince me that Jack and I aren't meant to be together.

"No is my least favorite word." He lifts his head too soon. "Let's go for a drive before I forget why burying my face between your legs and making you come until you stop blushing every time I look at you is a bad plan."

"Okay," I choke out.

Chapter Twelve

Jack

Providence, Rhode Island
2024

A SHORT TIME later, I'm seated in the passenger seat of
Cheryl's car. Its sleek design and its illuminated technology would be impressive if it wasn't so damn small. I'm
folded uncomfortably and forced to hunch over with my
elbows on my knees.

"You need to seatbelt yourself in," she says. "It's the law."

"A lap belt?" I crane my head around but don't immediately see one. Even if I did, I doubt there is a way to wrap it
around myself. "That's not currently feasible."

As if fully taking in my situation for the first time, she
makes a pained face. "You're bigger than I thought."

No man hates hearing that. I look away, smirk, meet her
gaze, but can't keep a straight face when I do.

She rolls her eyes, but smiles. "Try adjusting your seat

back."

"How?"

"Reach down on your right side. There are some buttons in the shape of the seat. Push them in the direction you want it to move."

I squeeze my hand between my seat and the car door. There are buttons, just as she said. I could figure out how to use them, but a better idea comes to me. My initial concern that she felt nothing for me is gone. More than once I've caught her looking at me with the same longing I feel for her. It's no longer a question of *if* we will be together, but rather *how* to get her comfortable around me. "On the door?"

"No, on your seat."

"Are you sure they're there?"

She unbuckles her belt. "I'm sure."

I shift to allow more room between my legs and chest as I pretend to stretch for these elusive buttons. "Are they large or small?"

"Hang on, I'll get out and come around."

"Or . . . you could reach over me."

The air stills.

Those little white teeth of hers sink into her plump bottom lip. She looks me over and flushes. God, she's beautiful.

I raise my arms out of the way.

She turns, gets on her knees and balances on one arm as she reaches over me. At first she's careful to not touch me, but her arm isn't long enough. She has to get closer. I inhale sharply when her breasts brush over my chest and down my side as she bends. I don't feel guilty in the least when that also proves to not be enough and she has to shift her body so she's more on me. "It's right here," she breathes out against my abdomen.

I bring my arms down, covering her seeking hand with mine while remembering how good it had felt earlier on my cock. "Here?"

"Yes."

I apply pressure to her fingers. My seat begins to move back and she wobbles above me. I place a hand on her hip to steady her.

"Better?" she asks.

"More," I growl as I fight the temptation to kiss every inch of her.

Her fingers move beneath mine and the top half of my seat tilts back. She slips. I bring both hands to her hips and easily lift her. A quick reposition on my part and she's straddling my lap, but forced forward onto me because of how little space there is.

I bring my arms around her and simply hug her. She's tense for a moment, but then relaxes onto me, her cheek on my chest, her hair splayed out over my arms. "Now we're cooking with gas."

She mumbles, "Why do I get the feeling you didn't need my help finding those buttons."

I chuckle. "Guilty as charged, but I did need this."

She tenses again. "Sex?"

I hug her closer. "In my day we called this making love."

"So sex."

I run my hand through her hair. It's not just the technology that has changed. Cheryl is more direct than I'm used to. I like it. "Making love is wooing someone—flirting—pitching for their affection."

"Oh. Nowadays it means—"

"Sex." I chuckle and kiss the top of her head. "I get it. But since you said you're trying not to do that anymore with men you don't know . . . this is us getting to know each other."

She raises her head and the irritation in her eyes is adorable. "Are you judging me for having been with other men?"

Her body fits against mine perfectly. God, the urge to tear our clothing off and claim her right now is so strong I shudder beneath her. "I don't have a problem with not being your first."

There's desire in her eyes, but also caution. "Because we're not in a relationship."

I trace a thumb over her parted lips. "I don't want to say you're wrong on our first day together, but . . ."

She shifts so she's sitting up, and the move rubs her sex over my throbbing cock. I don't try to hold back my moan of pleasure. Her hands go to my shoulders. I can't bring my head down to reach hers, not at this angle. She'll have to come to me.

"Friends first." She searches my face. "Isn't that what you said?"

I lift her again and raise her up until her face hovers over mine. She's still holding on to my shoulders as if there's a chance in hell I'll drop her. "Friends don't have sex in 2024?" Her mouth keeps opening and shutting like she has a lot to say but keeps deciding against sharing it. She wants me but she's not ready. I kiss her open lips lightly, then lower her back onto my lap. "Talk to me, Cheryl. What do you want?"

She looks down at my chest long enough that I start to worry I've offended her. When she speaks, it's in a low tone and with her gaze still lowered. "There is a high probability that everything you think you feel toward me is the result of a chemical reaction."

"It could be."

She sucks in an audible breath.

I continue, "It could be the same with you. You might really have a thing for spoons and any spoon will do. I could walk in one day and find you in bed rolling around with a ladle between your legs."

She covers her face with both hands. "I want to tell you that is ridiculous and could never happen, but we both know how I brought you back."

"So, you're ladle-curious?"

She lowers her hands and meets my gaze. "No."

"Are you sure?"

Irritation furrows her eyebrows. "I'm sure."

I cup one side of her face again. "I'm just as sure that what I feel is specific to you. You're mine, Cheryl. And I'm yours. I don't know how or why, but the reason I don't care about your past is because I'm your future." Her eyes are wide and anxious and I'm reminded of how Ray looked the night I found him taking drugs. "What are you afraid of?"

"Nothing."

"I was hoping you'd be honest."

She huffs in displeasure. "I am a well-educated, independent, modern woman. Nothing scares me."

"Except?"

Her back straightens and her whole body stiffens. "All I'm saying is that you can keep that whole 'I'm yours and you're mine' rhetoric to yourself. I don't need it or want it."

"Oh, okay. Independence is important to you."

"It is. I'll help you. I might even fuck you. But I don't need you."

I nod slowly as I begin to understand her. "I see. In this time, needing people is a bad thing?"

She gives me a long look as if trying to assess if I'm mocking her or not. "Yes . . . no . . . often. Listen, I'm not a spokesperson for the entire human race. I only know my own experience and what I'm willing to risk."

"Risk." Her word choice was revealing. "Because men have disappointed you in the past—failed to protect you?"

"Protect?" She laughs without humor. "Oh, Jack, the days when men protected women are far gone."

"I don't believe that."

"Well, I'm sorry to be the one to break it to you. If you fell down in the street, most people today would step over you and film themselves as they do."

"Would you do that?"

She shakes her head.

"Do you believe you're the last good person on the planet?"

"Of course not."

"Then maybe you shouldn't give up on humanity so easily." I run my hands up and down her back gently. "Or men."

Her eyes darken. "You sound amazing and I want to believe you, but you're too perfect. You're exactly what . . ." Her face turns red again.

My hands still. "I'd go over all the reasons I'm far from perfect, but I'm afraid I might disappear again."

Her hand fists with my shirt in it. "Don't go."

"I'll do my best not to." I take a deep breath before saying, "When I was young and blind, I resented how much I relied on those around me. I thought needing someone meant I was weak. War taught me that everyone bleeds . . . everyone needs . . . and the world can be scary as hell, so it's best to not face it alone."

She shudders and my cock takes that as an invitation to

harden eagerly. I shift beneath her as I wait for her response. She looks down into my eyes, into my very soul, and her yearning adds fuel to my own. "I want this to be real."

"I'm willing to believe in you if you're willing to believe in me." Deciding it might be time to lighten the mood a little, I suggest, "All you have to do is say my favorite word."

It only takes her a heartbeat to understand and a small smile pulls at her lips. "Yes?"

My hands move lower and cup her rear. "That's the one."

"Yes," she whispers.

"Do you still want to go for a drive?"

Her tongue darts across her lower lip. "Is that a trick question?"

"I'd rather tour your body than the city." I move my hand up to her hips. "But you should be the one to decide."

She didn't have to say a word . . . what she wanted was right in her eyes and in the way she scrambled off me and out of the car.

Okay, then.

Chapter Thirteen

Cheryl

Providence, Rhode Island
2024

Taking Jack by the hand and leading him to my bedroom felt natural and . . . necessary. But now that we're in my bedroom, I'm having flashbacks of our earlier encounters on my bed and, honestly, I'm panicking a little. I step a few feet away.

He's beside me with a speed that's also unsettling. "Are you okay?"

My breathing comes faster and harder, but not because I'm turned on. "I'm sorry. I'm freaking out a little. You're a spoon. A fucking spoon."

"That is unfortunately something I cannot deny."

I start pacing back and forth. "I've never had sex with a spoon." I stop because that's not accurate. "Other than you." Of course I haven't because having sex with a spoon is insane.

His expression gentles. "We don't have to do this."

"The problem is I want to."

He presses his lips together as if fighting back a smile. "The female mind is a complex and wondrous place I don't fully understand."

Hands on hips, I admit the issue. "I can't stop imagining you as a spoon and it's wigging me out."

"Oh." He pulls his shirt up and over his head, exposing a wide, muscled chest. "Does this help?"

My mouth goes dry and the embarrassment that met me at my bedroom door begins to fade. "A little." He's gorgeous. Every damn inch he exposes as he strips is toned. I notice a white line across one of his legs.

"Landmine. Large wounds heal, but they leave scars."

I nod, afraid if I ask him a question, he'll relive what must have been a horrific experience and disappear again. At least I know how to bring him back. I groan when a question bursts out of me that bypasses my filter. "Have you ever been in love?"

He pins me with one of his intense looks. "No, and truth be told, it's been a long time since I've been with a woman."

"Eighty years," I try to lighten the awkwardness with a joke.

"Eighty-three."

My mouth drops open. "That's a long time." Especially since he looks to be about my age.

His eyes darken and his expression becomes protective again. "We weren't sure it would be safe."

"Safe?" I swallow hard.

"We all have increased strength. I can lift a tank with my bare hands."

"Oh."

"None of us wanted to accidentally kill a woman."

"That seems like a . . . kind decision." Holy shit. Of all the things circling in my head, like if I could get pregnant from a spoon, I hadn't considered my death as a possible outcome. "Do you mind if I text Mercedes real quick?"

I sprint to where I left my phone in the living room and send Mercedes some pretty direct questions. Is sex safe? Do I need to take any precautions? When she says it is and suggests a simple condom, I replace the phone and head back to the bedroom. Jack is seated on the corner of my bed.

I announce, "We're good. I mean, be careful, but they've been having sex and Mercedes is very much alive."

His grin is slow and sinfully sexy. "Come here."

I move to stand before him. Seated, he's only slightly shorter than I am. I want him so badly. What's holding me back?

He studies my face. "Someone hurt you. Recently."

"No." I don't know what I expected a World War II super soldier to be like, but I hadn't thought he'd be so intuitive.

"You're lying to me again." He tips his head to one side.

"Or to yourself. I can't tell which."

I inhale sharply. "It was nothing."

"Tell me." He takes one of my hands in his and nothing in my life has ever felt so right.

Angry tears fill my eyes. "Don't."

"Don't what?"

"I handled it."

"What? What did you handle?" He cups my chin in his big hand and raises my eyes to his. "What happened, Cheryl?"

Shame floods in. I don't want to look him in the eye, but he holds my face immobile when I try to turn away. "It was my fault. I shouldn't have gone to a bar alone."

His hand tightens slightly on my chin. "Tell me exactly what he did."

The tears I hadn't allowed myself to release when it happened began to stream down my face. My voice thickens. "He slipped a drug in my drink. Thankfully I knew right away and confronted him. He took off. The bartender helped me get a car to take me home."

His touch turns gentle. "Where did this happen?"

I tell him the name of the bar. "It's one I've been to a few times because it's near my apartment. Thankfully, nothing really bad happened."

"Bad enough. He drugged you. And scared you."

I sniff. "I went to the police about it, but I don't know if they found him or if he's out there drugging some other woman. I want to go back to that bar and make sure he's not still there . . . but . . ."

"You're afraid to." His thumb gently massages my jaw.

"Not much of a badass, am I?" My face tightens as tears threaten again—and I'm not a crier. "I'm sorry."

"Don't be." He pulls me across his lap and wraps his strong arms around me.

My hands fist. "Ever feel like there are two versions of you? Sometimes I feel strong, independent, and free. And sometimes I'm scared and alone."

"Hey, it's okay." He kisses my lips gently then rests his forehead on mine. "I get it. I might look calm on the outside, but I don't want to be a spoon again and I don't know if I can control that."

I wipe the tears from my face and meet his gaze. "I must sound ridiculous. You're dealing with . . . *a lot* . . . and here I am all weepy over something that didn't even happen."

"Trauma is not a competition. Pain is pain." His arms tighten around me. "Stop being ashamed of feeling it. And don't allow it to isolate you. You're not alone anymore, Cheryl. If someone comes for you, they'll have to get through me."

I shiver as his words heal a part of me I've been struggling with for a long time. A memory returns of being tormented in elementary school by a bunch of students who accused me of thinking I was smarter than they were. They made my life a living hell until I stopped raising my hand.

Oh, my God, I gave them the power to silence me back then. Then I let them shape almost every decision I made after that.

"Talk to me, Cheryl."

What I just realized pours out of me. I don't stop until I share all of it—how I've held myself back academically as well as socially. "I gave them the power to define who I am."

Jack listens without interrupting. When I finish, he tucks my head under his chin and murmurs. "I know exactly how that feels. I guess the question we need to ask ourselves is . . . what will we become now that we're free of them?"

Yeah. "Less afraid."

"That's a good place to start."

For the first time, I wrap my arms around him and hug him tightly. "You're not alone either, Jack. I'll help you figure out what happened to you and how to come back on your own. I swear I will."

He tips his head back and there's a sparkle in his eyes. "I don't mind the current method, but I would like to not feel trapped when I revert to a spoon."

"Well, lucky for you, you have a girlfriend who loves to research things."

"Is that what you are? My girlfriend?"

The look of pleasure in his expression gives me the confidence to say, "I don't know what else to call myself. Spoon master?"

He barks out a laugh then rolls with me until I'm pinned

beneath him in the middle of my bed. "Master. We'll have to take turns with that position."

I run my hands over his bare chest. "I'm thinking of a word. It has three letters."

Balancing his weight on his elbows, he runs his hands through my hair and murmurs, "I hope it's my favorite word."

I slide a hand down his muscled stomach to cup his impressively large manhood. "Yes?"

His cock jerks against my hand. "That's the one."

He rolls again and I'm above him, straddling him. "Do you mind if I undress you, ma'am?" His tone is playful.

I'm so used to men rushing to what they consider the good part that I'm taken aback. "Um, sure."

He lifts me as if I weigh nothing and repositions himself against the headboard of my bed before placing me once again in a straddle position across his lap. "I've had sex . . ."

I chuckle nervously. "That's a relief."

He taps a finger lightly on my nose. "But never as a sighted man."

"Oh."

"So, if it's alright with you, I'd like to take my time and get to know every inch of you."

I clear my throat. "That sounds nice."

He lifts my shirt up and over my head. I'm wearing a practical sports bra because this wasn't how I imagined the day going. He doesn't seem the least bit disappointed. His hands come up to cup my breasts through the material. My nipples harden at the attention. "So beautiful."

I can't take any more; I pull my bra off and toss it to the side. His rough hands on my bare skin is sheer heaven. I've never considered myself particularly attractive, but I feel young and sexy beneath his adoring gaze.

Our eyes meet and we share a laugh. How a man can be as sexy and strong as he is while still remaining sweet is beyond me. And my ability to think about anything beyond how good being with him feels is quickly diminishing.

He lifts me until I'm standing with one foot on each side of his thighs. With anyone else, the kind of strength he has might be intimidating, but I want to be moved around by him. He's undressing me like I'm a present, his to unwrap. And that's how I feel.

He slides off my shoes, my pants, then my panties. I'm naked before him, and should feel vulnerable, but instead I feel powerful. He wants me, needs me. He's mine.

"I want to see you before I taste you."

It's an unusual request and I'm not entirely sure what it entails, but I whisper his favorite word and am rewarded with a smile. His hands cup my ass then move lower to grip my thighs. I teeter slightly as he lifts me until my sex is slightly higher than his face, then he parts my legs and I unfold for his view. "So fucking perfect."

"Thank you," I murmur, unsure of what a woman is supposed to say in response to that.

His tongue flicks out and the length of it takes my breath away. It reaches clear to the back of my ass and tastes every inch of me, back to front in a bold move that has me gripping his shoulders and closing my eyes.

The tip of his tongue circles my clit, strong and nimble like a finger. Back and forth, around and around, he drives me nearly out of my mind. Every time I think it might be too much, he claims the entirety of me again and I spread my legs wider.

I could marry that tongue of his. Bear its children. Belong to that part of him alone. God, the things he can do with it. I'm writhing in his hands, mewling for him.

And then . . .

Then that huge, talented tongue of his thrusts upward into me and I scream as I orgasm. But he doesn't stop. It doesn't stop. It moves in and out of me, filling me, tasting me, owning me. It's hot, wet, slick as hell, and knows exactly where my G-spot is. I'm his for the taking, powerless to do anything but come again while I sob his name because his tongue demands nothing less than my complete submission.

I'm sweaty and limp when he lowers me to my feet again and turns me around. One strong hand across my back bends me in front of his face. His breath warms my ass before his hands part my cheeks.

His tongue snakes toward my sex and I brace myself for whatever his pleasure is. It plunges back into my sex, filling me, pumping in and out as his hands come around to twist my nipples lightly.

I'm about to come for, I can't believe it, but, the third time when he lifts me again and puts me to one side. I can't take my eyes off him. He's more endowed than any man I've been with, but I'm ready for it.

"Get on your knees," he orders.

I drop eagerly. He buries his hands in my hair and dips the tip of his cock into my mouth. Just the tip. His expression is pained and I can tell he's being careful with me. I open my mouth as wide as I can and do my best to accommodate most of him. It's not humanly possible to, but I've learned a few tricks of my own along the way.

I encircle him with one hand and work him with both hand and mouth. I tease his balls, hoping to bring him even half the pleasure he's brought me. Deeper and deeper I take him, until breathing becomes difficult. He doesn't thrust as some men do. He lets me move around him and I love how his hands tighten in my hair the more excited he becomes.

"Stop," he growls, pulling out of my mouth. "Turn around again."

I rise to my feet and do as he ordered. He grips my hips and lifts me. I'm Superman flying in front of him, with my legs around his waist. He takes me like that, entering me from behind, and holds me there, a good thing because my body needs time to adjust to the length and girth of him. I might have imagined it, but I could have sworn his cock adjusted to a size I could handle.

The restrained power of him is excruciatingly sexy. I want to cry out for him to let go and ravage me, but I also want to stay alive to do this again.

In and out.

Deeper and harder.

Fuller and fuller.

I'm stretched to capacity when he begins to thrust into me harder and harder. Faster and faster. I don't have control of the situation. He withdraws, turns me, and begins to fuck me from the front. He's too powerful to fully hold on to. I'm just along for the ride, but what a ride it is.

When he comes inside me I feel it. I don't know if his sperm is shaped normal or like a little cutlery army and I don't care. I collapse against his chest. I'm his and he's mine and that's all that matters.

He carries me to the shower and begins to wash me. "Am I dirty?" I joke.

He kisses me deeply, so well and for so long I can't remember if I asked a question. Then he lathers me up and enjoys washing me down. "Just returning the favor," he whispers in my ear.

He dries me then carries me back to my bed, lies down beside me, and curls around my back. I want to make a spooning joke, but it feels too soon.

"Was that good?" he asks, kissing my neck.

My answer is a word that is quickly becoming my favorite as well.

Chapter Fourteen

Jack

Providence, Rhode Island
2024

W<small>HEN</small> I <small>WAKE</small>, Cheryl has turned in my arms and is looking at me. "Hi."

"Hi." Her smile starts in her eyes and I've never seen anything more beautiful. Amazingly enough, she blushes beneath my attention.

"How can you still be shy around me?" I ask.

Her hand splays across my chest. "Even though it doesn't feel that way, there's a lot we don't know about each other."

She's right. "Ask me anything."

"How do you feel about being here . . . in this time period? Not here in my bed."

Of course Cheryl would ask a question I didn't yet know the answer to. "Conflicted, I guess."

"Because you wish you could go back?"

I kiss her forehead before answering, stalling long enough to figure out how to express what I'm feeling. Cheryl isn't just a woman I had sex with. She feels like a part of me now. An essential part. I don't know that I'd choose to go back if I were given the chance to. Not now. "I'm where I belong, but I don't like how I left things with my family. When you spoke earlier of changing who you were to please your schoolmates, I said I understood because I also changed for someone I shouldn't have given the power to shape me."

"The government?"

"My father."

"Did he sign you up for the program?"

"No. He didn't think enough of me to believe I could handle battle."

"I don't understand."

I normally preferred to not talk about my family, but I want her to know me. "I thought serving my country would finally prove to my father that I'm good enough to be considered his first son. I chose chasing the approval of a man who never loved me over staying and caring for a mother who always put my needs before her own."

"Why do you think your father didn't love you?"

"He was a strong man—one of action over words. I was born blind. Helpless . . . worthless to him."

She snuggles closer. "I'm so sorry."

"My mother more than made up for what he lacked. I never wanted for anything. She made sure I had an Ivy

League education. She filled my life with people who taught me how to survive, but she couldn't make my father accept me." I breathe and distance myself from the pain I'm afraid will consume me and revert me to a spoon. "I hate that I didn't choose to stay with her. Protect her. Repay her for all she did for me. There's so much I would have said to her had I known I'd never see her again. I was born into a vulnerable position, but never felt helpless because she taught me how not to be. I never thanked her for that."

"I'm sure you did—by being a son she was proud of."

"I hope so."

"Did she know about the experiments?"

"She did. I snuck out to meet with her. I don't know if that makes it better or worse. The families of the rest of my unit believed their sons were dead. Mine knew I was alive— and I promised her I'd be back. She believed me."

"We could find out what happened to her. Possibly right now."

I tense. "How?"

"Remember that phone you said you'd let me show you how to use? It's also a computer that is wirelessly attached to many other computers around the world via something called the internet."

"The internet?"

"Yes. Imagine a pool of information everyone is able to access."

"With a phone."

"With computers in general, but yes also phones."

"And you can show me how to do this?"

"Absolutely. I'm a research-aholic so I know my way around public record sites. I can't promise anything, but there's a high likelihood that in less than an hour we could know more about your family than I know about my own."

"Like if my brother made it home from war?"

"That one is probably one of the easiest to find."

"And my parents? I'd like to know what happened to them."

"Counties keep records of births, deaths, marriages, and home sales. We can learn a lot in a short amount of time." Her smile is gentle. "But you'll have to let me up so I can get our phones."

I nuzzle her neck then give her lips a quick kiss. "I do want the information, but it is hard to let you go."

She chuckles, kisses me, then wriggles free. "I'll be right back."

The view of her naked ass sashaying away is worth being without her for a few minutes. When she returns, I sit up and invite her to settle between my legs with her back to my chest. She dives right in. I pull a blanket up to warm her, even though the sight of her is something I know I'll never tire of.

She holds up one small device and says, "This is my phone." She hands me a similar one. "This is yours. The first thing I'll show you is how to turn it on."

My dick jerks against her back.

Stand down, she wasn't talking about you.

She shimmies closer against me and I'm no longer sure my dick wasn't right.

She continues, "Did you see how I turned mine on? Do the same to yours."

I shake my head. Phone. We're talking about the phones.

She glances up at me. "I'll shut mine down and start it up again. This time, pay attention."

I chuckle and kiss her bare shoulder. "I'm trying. Maybe if you stop moving I can focus on what you're saying instead of how much I want to fuck you again."

Her mouth rounds. "Oh." Then she laughs. "Should I put some clothes on?"

I growl and shift her back more until my erect cock is nestled between her cheeks. "No, this is good."

"It is," she murmurs, then slaps my thigh lightly. "Now watch, this is how you turn your phone on."

"The *phone*," I echo.

Learning how to use this new technology might take a very long time.

Chapter Fifteen

Cheryl

Providence, Rhode Island
2024

I DECIDE TO start with Jack. When I can't find any record of his birth or death, he explains he hasn't used his real name since before signing up for Project Inkwell. The record of Jackson Chatfield's death matches when he said the government would have faked his.

We look up his father next. Jack doesn't seem upset at the news that he didn't survive the war. He died in a convoy explosion and is buried in Arlington.

Relief visibly floods through Jack when we find discharge papers for his brother, Paul, and then a death certificate that is dated many years later. We're both smiling when I'm able to find photos of Paul at his wedding and even some with their mother.

"That's Farley," Jack says as he points to an older man

who seems to be next to his mother in every photo.

"Who was he?"

Jack sighs. "More of a father to me than mine ever was. He took good care of my mother as well."

I do a quick search and bounce with joy. "Looks like he married her."

Jack grabs my phone and shudders. "He married her." When he sniffs, I crane my neck to see his face. His eyes shine with emotion. "Good for you, Farley. Good for you."

He hands the phone back and I show him how to search for more information about them. Photos and records become easier to find as our search takes us through the decades.

"Your brother had two children," I say as I scan a genealogy site. "Named Timothy and Daisy. They both married and had children. Neither are still alive, but their children are. One is in Montana and one is . . . in Connecticut. Not too far away. We could drive to meet that one when you're ready."

"Cheryl, I don't think you understand how much this means to me." His arms wrap around me and nearly squeeze the breath out of me. "Thank you."

"You're welcome."

He kisses my shoulder again. "There are some things I need to do before I visit anyone. First, it's necessary to ensure that it's safe to."

Fear shivers down my back. "You're right to be careful.

Someone might still want you dead."

He lets out a heavy sigh. "Everything they did to us, everything *we* did . . . it all felt worth it when we thought we were saving the world. If you knew what we did—"

"I don't care."

"You should. I am happier with you than I remember ever being, but I can't help but ask myself if I deserve to be. Farley did. He was never anything but a good man." He inhales deeply. "But me? Maybe I earned the prison they trapped me in."

I turn and go onto my knees, my hand cupping his face. "You were lied to during an ugly time in history. You did what you thought you had to do. And you did save us. We're all still here because of men like you and the sacrifices you made."

"But was it worth the cost? All those civilians . . ."

I raise and lower my shoulders. I don't have the words to console him for that one. I doubt anyone does. But I don't think he deserved what happened to him.

Looking to cheer him, I change the topic to all the good ways the world has changed since 1945. We get lost in YouTube videos on history, travel, current technology as well as what's expected in the near future.

Between the videos, he tells me about his life, his family, and the missions he was sent on. We talk about the other men in his unit, the ones who died early and the ones he's hoping are in the silverware.

My life feels dull in comparison, but that doesn't stop him from asking a slew of questions about it. As we talk, my perspective shifts. My parents always pushed me to excel. I viewed that as them not thinking I was good enough.

However, listening to Jack talk about how Farley consistently pushed for Jack to be able to protect himself and be independent makes me wonder if that isn't exactly what my parents have been trying to do for me.

Not to change me, but to guide me.

Late into the night, Jack scrolls through a variety of social media platforms. "Do people share every part of their lives online?"

"Everything they want people to see."

He stops on a video that looks like it's taken from above the person delivering a package. "Why do so many look like they don't know they're being filmed?"

"Oh, because there are cameras everywhere now. People put them on their homes. Businesses put them inside and outside. I assume someone is always either watching or listening."

"So, how does crime still exist?"

"People find a way." I sigh. "They cover their faces, wear hoods . . . criminals always find a way."

"I see. What could be listening to us now?"

I shrug. "I try not to think about it too much, but probably my phone. Also anything that connects to the internet could." He murmurs something behind me, but too low for me to understand. "It's not really an issue. I have nothing to hide." His stillness behind me has me rethinking that last claim. "Unless someone starts looking for you."

Neither of us speak for a few minutes.

Eventually, he murmurs, "Show me something most people wouldn't expect you to be into."

I bite my bottom lip then reach over to the drawer beside my bed. "For that, I'll need a different device."

When I hold up what I retrieved, he looks at it with interest. "What is it?"

"A Kindle."

"What does it do?"

I swipe to open to my library and show him my extensive collection of romance novels. "It brings me joy—a lot of joy."

With his chin on my shoulder, he scans the book covers. "Virgin for the Trillionaire?" His voice is full of humor.

"Oh, that's an older book." I swipe down.

"The Beast Loves Curves?"

I swipe again. "I am a closet romance reader and you're the one who asked me to show you something most people wouldn't know about me."

His arms wrap tighter around me. "I didn't mean to embarrass you. I'm trying to get to know you. What are these books about?"

"Love. Hate. Friendship. Family. And a lot of sex."

"Oh." I feel his smile against my cheek. "I may want a

Kindle of my own."

"Or we could share mine." God, I love how easy it is to be with him. It shouldn't be. We haven't known each other more than a day, but that's not how it feels.

"I'd like that." He nuzzles my neck. "I'd like that a lot."

I turn so our mouths meet and everything else fades away. His past, any danger that might be lurking, or what tomorrow might hold for us . . . none of it matters. I toss my Kindle to the side and turn so I'm on my knees between his legs.

I'm his.

He's mine.

The rest will just have to figure itself out.

Chapter Sixteen

Jack

IN THE MORNING, Cheryl is sound asleep and snoring when I slip out of her bed. Unable to resist, I bend and kiss her gently on the lips before I force myself to leave her side and gather my clothing. I would tell her where I'm going, but if things in her home really do listen in, it's better if I say nothing. I call Hugh for his address. He offers to pick me up at the apartment, but I don't want to involve Cheryl in what I have planned for the day. He tells me there is an app on my phone that will call a car to me and bring me to his place. It takes a bit of explaining on his part, but I'm able to do it and secure transportation.

I leave my phone behind and go downstairs to meet the car. It comes, just as the phone said it would. I fold my large frame into the backseat of the small car.

The driver is a young, bearded man and with a cap on backward. His smile is cheerful. "You a football player?" he asks.

"No."

"Basketball?"

"No."

"If I were your size I'd be in the big leagues of some sport."

I look out the window and hope he'll stop speaking if I stop responding. Some of the buildings look similar to how they did in my time, but the people on the streets don't. Everything is louder, busier, and more complicated. When I'm with Cheryl she's all I can think about. Distance from her is giving me the time and clarity of thought to wonder if she wouldn't be better off without me.

I didn't sleep last night. Instead, I lay there thinking about how I'd gotten there and how Ray's last words had been that he was sorry. I need answers from him as well as Hugh. But, first, I need to deal with the man who drugged Cheryl. Hugh's been here longer than I have. He'll know how to track him down.

After parking in front of Mercedes' apartment building, the driver reminds me to leave him a good review. I say I will even though I have no idea what that means.

Hugh meets me in the lobby of the building. I ask him if he has his phone with him. He does. I tell him to turn it off and follow me outside. He does both without hesitation.

"I'm glad you're here," he says. "I have a lot to catch you up on."

He falls into step with me. "Do you know how we became silverware?"

"Not yet."

"Do you know if Project Inkwell still exists in any form? Are they out there conducting research on other men?"

"I don't know."

My hands fist at my sides. "Then what the fuck do you know, Hugh? What have you been doing with your time here?"

His face blanches like I physically hit him. "We can't go back, Jack. Our goal now should be to free our unit and set them up with a life in this time period. All of them will need what we gave you—a new identity. We've been given a second chance."

I side-eye him. "How are you not furious that someone did this to us?"

"I was." He sighs. "But once you get used to it, life is not bad in the future. You'll feel the same a few weeks from now."

I spin on him, grabbing the collar of his shirt. "No, I won't. Someone took everything from me and I will find out who it was." Realizing I'm venting my anger on someone who had done nothing to earn it, I release his collar. "Our new mission needs to be to make sure no one is out there doing to anyone else what was done to us."

Hugh adjusts his shirt. He's not angry, which means he at least partly agrees with me. "Before we do that, we need to free the rest of our unit, and, so far, that's not a quick process."

"You still can't control when you come back?"

"No. Only when I revert to a fork. I can choose that."

"If we can do it one way, the reverse has to be possible."

"I haven't found that to be true yet, but I haven't given up on the idea. It might have something to do with female pheromones or some chemical reaction within us in response to an aroused woman."

"So, you have put thought into this."

"Of course."

I rub a hand over my chin. "I feel attached to Cheryl—not just physically. I can't imagine feeling this way for another woman."

He nods. "It's the same for me with Mercedes. At first, I was afraid the intensity would fade, but my feelings have only gotten stronger. I love her—more than I ever thought I could love anyone."

"None of this makes sense."

"No, it doesn't."

"But I believe you because, if I were offered the chance to go back in time, I don't know if I would want to if that meant leaving Cheryl."

Hugh lets out an audible breath. "That feeling gets stronger and stronger the longer you're here. I'm not saying I don't care about tracking down what happened to Falcon and the others . . . I just care about Mercedes more."

"You mean that. Shit. I need to get some business done before I feel the same."

"What are you talking about?"

"There's a man I need your help tracking down. I don't know his name or much about him. I know what he looks like, where Cheryl met him, and what he did to her. You and I are going to find him today and neutralize his potential to ever hurt another woman."

"What did he do?"

"Not as much as he hoped, but enough that he reminds me a little too much of some of the scum we came across in Germany. With strength comes responsibility. If the police don't already have him, let's resolve that problem for them."

Hugh grabs one of my arms and pulls me to a stop. "I didn't agree with what you and Ray did in Germany. You're only a man and not meant to be judge, jury, and execution-er. You shouldn't have been back then, and it's too dangerous for you to be that here. I won't allow it."

I shake his hand off and snarl. "*Allow it?* You think you're still in charge? Let's get something straight right now—you're not. I will track this scum down with or without you. He came after my woman. I won't let him come for her twice—or any other innocent. Either join me and help me do it without being noticed or stay out of my way."

Hugh emits a low growl. "We're on the same team."

"Then prove it."

"I don't like this."

I bend so we're nose to nose. "Get that judgmental look off your mug. Your hands aren't cleaner than mine because you only acted when following orders. Evil is evil. I may go to hell for what I'm about to do, but I'm going to make sure that bastard is already there waiting to greet me."

"I can't let you do this alone—so, okay. I'm in. We'll find him."

"Yes, we will." We start walking again. "And then we need to talk about who we should free next."

"No. Not him. Not yet."

"He knows something, Hugh. I feel it in my bones."

"That's why he should be the last one we free."

"I want answers."

"We'll get them, but in time, when we can handle them . . . and him."

I could argue my point more, but it's best to focus on one operation at a time. "Do you have a car we can take?"

"Mercedes does."

"Can we trust her?"

"Without question."

We turn around and head back to their apartment. Mercedes meets us at the door, holding a cat that hisses at me before she puts it on the floor.

Hugh says, "Mercedes, I need your help. I can't tell you

what it is. You can never ask me about it later and we're going to hurt someone."

Without missing a beat, Mercedes says, "I'll get my keys." She pauses and jokes. "And, Hugh, you need to stop watching so many movies. You're starting to sound like them."

They exchange a laugh and the expression on both of their faces gives me pause. The attachment goes both ways and that knowledge sends a heady amount of hope through me. Will Cheryl and I have that? My heart tells me we will.

My head warns me that if I'm not careful I might lose everything I care about . . . again.

Chapter Seventeen

Cheryl

Providence, Rhode Island
2024

WAKE ALONE, which shouldn't feel odd because it's how I always wake. As the events of the last day fill my groggy mind, it's easy to wonder if any or all of it was a dream. Knowing my life, being drugged by a stranger at a bar was probably the last thing that actually happened.

I don't usually remember dreams as vividly as I do this one. I roll over, bury my face in my pillow, and groan as my mind replays the highlights of it.

I fucked a spoon?

And then a super soldier.

Jack.

God, he was good in bed—definitely raised the bar for all sex dreams in the future. Hear that, subconscious me, if you can't deliver a quality romp like that again, don't even bother.

I stretch as I wake more and realize I'm naked. I suppose that makes sense since I remember cleaning vomit from my rug naked.

And then the police station.

And going to see Mercedes to return the spoon.

And then talking to Ashley about it.

Oh, shit, none of that was a dream.

I sit up and look around. Jack was beside me when I fell asleep. Where is he now? I listen for a sound from the bathroom or outside of my bedroom. Nothing.

I crawl out of bed and slip on a T-shirt and shorts. Jack's uniform is neatly folded in a pile on the corner of my bureau with his boots on the floor below. I didn't imagine him, but I am disappointed that he's not with me. I check the time. Ugh. I should have been at work hours ago. A quick phone call to my supervisor during which I deepen my voice and claim I woke with a stomach bug ends with me having a couple of days off. That's the perk of living a boring life and having never called in. Everyone knows I don't party or do anything exciting enough to keep me out of work, so my claim of raging diarrhea and throwing up is taken at face value.

I find Jack's phone on the end table near my couch. He's still here. Shit, is he a spoon again? Finding a good man is tough, but I never imagined doing this. I scour my apartment, every room, under all the furniture, even remove the cushions from my couch. I even check my silverware drawer and dishwasher because . . . well, dating a spoon doesn't come with instructions. I don't know if he sleeps in a bed or feels more comfortable in a drawer.

Part of being in a relationship is accepting the other person's differences. This is definitely different.

I'm not going to judge. After all, I *did* orgasm with him back when he was still a utensil. I don't know if I was ever normal, but I certainly can't make that claim anymore.

As I look at all the silverware in my kitchen drawer, I worry that I won't be able to eat with any of them anymore without feeling like I'm cheating on Jack. I remember feeling strongly about not wanting him to feel that he belongs to me just because I brought him back.

The ache that fills me from imagining my life without him . . . it's beyond what I could express in words or justify if asked to. We bonded. He's not just my spoon; he's the only spoon I'll ever want in my mouth or anywhere else on my body.

Vibrators? My man can become one. How many women can claim that?

Crazy.

Wild.

But undeniable.

He is mine.

And I am his.

I pace from room to room. He's not here, but his phone

is. I've never been the type to want to check the phone of any man. I've always thought if I got to that point with anyone we were already in a bad enough place that whatever I found wouldn't matter. This is different. Jack could be lost, hurt, or both.

The last call he made was to Hugh. That makes sense. They're friends and they haven't had time to talk yet. Is that where he is? With Hugh?

I wish Jack had woken me. I would have gladly driven him over to see Hugh. God, if Ashley and I ended up eighty years in the future together, I can imagine needing to decompress with her on a regular basis. I may claim to understand what Jack is going through, but Hugh actually does.

I send Mercedes a text from my phone. For my sanity, I want to confirm that Jack is with them and safe. She doesn't answer.

Now what?

I check which apps Jack has open and see that he used a rideshare service. Okay. Destination? Mercedes' place. The ride was completed and paid for. I take a deep breath and return Jack's phone to where I found it.

Part of me wants to text Mercedes again, but I don't. I refuse to be that clingy. Jack survived World War II, he doesn't need my help to get around the capital of the smallest state in the union.

Even if the government might still be looking for him,

and cameras now have facial recognition. Nope, I'm not going to overthink this.

My phone bings with an incoming text and I nearly drop it as I hastily fumble to check if it's from Mercedes. It's not.

It's Ashley.

Her: Text me when you're on break.

Me: I'm on break all day. I called in sick.

Her: Oh no. What kind of crud did you catch?

I'm not ready to tell her the truth, but I also don't want to lie.

Me: I just didn't feel like going in today

My phone instantly rings. "Want me to come to you? Do you want to come here? Are we watching old movies and pretending nothing happened or crying and binge eating? I just need to know what to wear."

I laugh. The rest of my life might be upside down, but I still have Ashley. "I'm fine."

"Don't believe that for a second. You never call in and you've told me you don't believe in taking healthy days out."

She knows me too well. "I wanted some time to work some things through."

"The job decision."

I hadn't put much thought into that, but sure. "It's a lot, but I'm okay."

"As long as you're sure. Technically, I am working today,

but I've trained my team to focus on the goals I meet and not how long my breaks are or aren't. There are strong scientific arguments for how dopamine can trigger creativity."

"Wait. Explain to me exactly how that works."

"Um. Okay. Dopamine tweaks your brain's alpha waves, especially in the prefrontal cortex, the anterior cingulate cortex, and the DMN."

I know this, but in my rush to remember, I need to hear it to be able to connect it to what I'm thinking. "How exactly?"

She chuckles. "Lucky for you, this is something I think about a lot because I'm always looking for ways to make the robots happier. Dopamine promotes alpha wave synchronization—making you more relaxed. It allows a person's thoughts to free flow easier, while remaining alert."

"And it's released during orgasm, right?"

"Technically, levels start to rise even during sexual anticipation and arousal, which is why my department consistently outperforms the rest of the company. I don't wear short skirts and button-down blouses for nothing. You're welcome."

"Hold on. Does dopamine interact with testosterone?"

"Sure does. It boosts testosterone production. The two are actually bidirectional when it comes to amplifying each other. When both are present, it creates a healthy feedback loop for the whole body."

"Testosterone diffuses through the cell membrane and binds to androgen receptors. I remember this. Then, the testosterone-androgen receptor complex translocates into the nucleus of the cells. Oh, my God, it can activate genes into mRNA and stimulate the production of proteins. It's the dopamine that's the trigger. It has to be. The dopamine starts a chain reaction, sending out a message that every cell needs to change—add that to whatever was done to make them heal quickly and that's how they're changing back and forth. It's why they revert when they're sad. I can't believe it took me this long to figure it out."

God, I love having smart friends.

"What are you talking about?"

"I'll explain later. I need to deep-dive into whatever research I can find on this topic. You're a genius, Ashley, and you may have helped a lot of people."

"Without even flashing my toned thighs. That's a first," she answers with a laugh. "Glad I could help."

"We'll talk later." Right before I end the call I say, "Oh, and do me a favor. Could you tell Greg and Leo to stop looking into Project Inkwell? I'll explain more when I see you, but it's better if we shelve that for now."

"Oh, no, is Mercedes being weird about it again?"

"No, actually. I was wrong about her, and I owe her an apology. I'll tell you all about that later too."

"I'd grill you more, but my supervisor's wife is heading toward my office. She doesn't appreciate my attire and she's convinced I'm after her man. I've tried to explain to her that round and bald isn't my taste, but she's territorial as fuck."

"Maybe invite Leo to come by? Let her see you with your guy."

"Ugh, we broke up."

"No."

"Yeah, it's your fault really. Once I imagined him as a teaspoon, I couldn't get the image out of my head. I don't even like tea. I thought being with someone was better than being lonely, but there has to be someone out there for me. I don't want to settle. I want to crave someone. I want someone to crave me. Is that so wrong?"

"No," I murmur. "That's not wrong at all."

We end the call and I take a moment to appreciate how lucky I am to have met Jack. No matter how things turn out, he's changed what I expect from a relationship. I don't want to sleep with men who don't care if they see me again. I'm done fucking people just to feel connected to them.

If things don't work out with Jack, I'd rather spend a lifetime alone than settle for less than what we have. And if he was ever mixed in with a pile of cutlery, I know I'd fuck a thousand . . . no, a million spoons if that's what it takes to find him again.

I hope that's not what it takes.

Chapter Eighteen

Jack

Providence, Rhode Island
2024

L ATER THAT DAY, Mercedes and Hugh are in the front
seats of her car as they drive me back to Cheryl's. I'm in
the back, enjoying that I can stretch out my legs for once. I
changed my clothes at their place because, although there's
not a mark on me, I didn't want to explain blood stains to
Cheryl.

Not on our second day together.

The giddiness that overtakes me as we park beside Cheryl's building is unsettling, but also amazing. I didn't think it
was possible to be this excited to be with anyone. Knowing
she'll be in my arms in a few minutes, my senses will fill with
the scent and feel of her. I close my eyes and savor the
anticipation.

"Get out, Loverboy," Hugh says.

I unfold myself onto the sidewalk. "Thanks for today."

He nods. "Do you want us to come in?"

I open my mouth to say no, but before I can utter a sound, Cheryl bursts out of the front door of the building. She pauses. I smile, start walking to her, and open my arms. We're like magnets, pulled helplessly toward each other until we meet with a mash of bodies and mouths. I lift her. She wraps her legs around my waist, and we step out of time together and into bliss.

Behind us, Hugh says, "We should go."

Mercedes' response is cheerful and oblivious. "We'll give them a minute, but I want to make sure Cheryl's okay."

"She looks okay to me."

Out of respect for both Cheryl and Mercedes, I reluctantly end the kiss and lower Cheryl back to her feet. Before releasing her, though, I say, "I missed you."

She gives my cheek a peck. "I'm glad I won't have to diddle a million spoons."

What? "Are you finding other spoons attractive?" I'd only been joking when I mentioned that possibility.

She laughs reassuringly. "No. Just you. Sorry, what I should have said was I missed you too."

I couldn't let go of the image of her with another spoon. "How do you feel about eating soup with a straw from now on?"

She tips her head to one side before answering. "I'll consider it, if you promise to wake me the next time you're heading out for the day without your phone. I don't care where you go. I was worried before I figured out you were with Hugh."

"Did my phone tell you that?"

"In a roundabout way, yes."

"I don't know if I want a phone. No one likes a rat."

Her eyes narrow ever so slightly. "You say that like you spent the day doing something illegal."

Mercedes sweeps in, links arms with Cheryl and pulls her away. I'm both grateful and impressed. Mercedes might be smarter than she lets on. She beams a smile at Cheryl. "So, you have a super soldier and I have a super soldier. Do you think Ashley would want one? Imagine how fun it would be to have that in common. We were friends before, but this kind of makes us sisters, don't you think?"

I don't know what I expected Cheryl's response to be, but she turns to Mercedes and gives her a long hug. Long enough that it takes Mercedes by surprise as well. When she's released, Mercedes asks, "Are you okay, Cheryl?"

Cheryl looks from Mercedes to me and back. "Mercedes, I wasn't the friend to you I should have been. I judged you harshly and I'm sorry."

Mercedes' smile doesn't waver. "I know. And, honestly, we're very different. You're super smart and I—"

"Don't say it." Cheryl puts her hands on Mercedes' shoulders and gives her a little shake. "I'm book smart, but I've been life-dumb until now. I didn't believe you when you told me about Hugh. I couldn't imagine a world in which things like that were possible. Today, I had a lot of time to think about why I was having such a hard time choosing between the job I have and the job my parents want me to take. And do you know what I realized?"

Her eyes meet mine and I hold my breath, knowing that her next words will reflect how she feels about me as well.

She continues, "I don't want to live in a world where only those two options are possible. I want to be surprised and challenged by things I don't understand. I want to do more than make money for people who are already rich." She holds out a hand to me and our fingers lace. "I want what life with Jack offers—whatever that is and wherever it takes us."

I raise her hand to my lips and kiss her knuckles. "Me too."

She turns back to Mercedes. "And I want to be someone who doesn't judge people as easily as I have in the past. You and I are not alike, Mercedes, but that doesn't make you any less remarkable. I'm lucky to have you as a friend, and I would love to think you, Ashley, and I could be sisters." She winks. "Warning, my parents are a snore fest, but they're good people."

"Mine too," Mercedes says before snuggling against Hugh's side and telling him, "But they'd love to meet all of you once you get full control of your transitions."

Cheryl hops like she was jolted. "Shit, I can't believe I

almost forgot. I think I figured out how you change back and forth. I'm not sure, but it's a theory that makes sense." She scans my face. "I could explain it over dinner if everyone wants to come in."

Hugh answers first. "Sounds perfect."

Perfect.

Dinner involves food and we all know what that involves. So instead of spending the next few hours tasting her, teasing her, on her and in her, I'll get to watch that sweet mouth of hers close around other utensils.

As if she could read my mind, Cheryl says, "I could make tacos or hamburgers. I don't know about you, but I'm giving up silverware for a while." When my eyes widen, she adds, "Outside of Jack."

"We're a purely plastic household," Mercedes chirps.

"And I appreciate that." Hugh kisses her cheek and I get it. This is uncharted territory for all of us.

"I'll invest in some." Cheryl meets my gaze again and there's no judgment in her eyes. She understands me as few ever did.

A black SUV slows down and parks across the street. I'm not sure why it catches my eye, but it does. There seems to be only one person in the car—the driver. As soon as I motion toward it, it pulls away and speeds off. I exchange a look with Hugh. If we weren't with the women, I would have taken off after it. He shakes his head ever so slightly and I decide he might be right. It could be nothing.

It didn't appear to be a police car.

Hugh and I had done everything we could to avoid cameras and we'd disposed of all evidence far outside the city limits. Still, whoever was in that car had hoped to watch us without being noticed.

I didn't like that.

"Let's go inside," I suggest.

Chapter Nineteen

Cheryl

Providence, Rhode Island
2024

IT'S A LAZY Sunday morning. Jack and Hugh are out for a jog.

I'm puttering around the spare room of my apartment, organizing all the lab equipment we've recently filled it with.

Time has never passed so quickly. I quit my job and am currently living off my savings, but Hugh has some money his family set aside for him and together we're assembling a makeshift lab in my apartment.

Mercedes doesn't know a vortex mixer from an orbital shaker, but her unwavering optimism bolsters my faith that together we can help free the other men. Not just free them from being silverware, but also from the need to have a woman be part of the process.

Neither Hugh nor Jack think that's necessary, but I want

Jack to be with me because he chooses to be, not because he's chemically dependent on my presence. He assures me that's not what our bond is, but the scientist in me wants to give him all the answers, not just the ones that best serve me.

What's the saying? If you love a spoon set it free . . . or something like that.

Jack has learned to control when he reverts to a spoon, but he still can't come back without assistance. The more time I spend with him, the more I realize that loving him is different than owning him. Lust is easy. It can be obsessive, controlling, and jealous. Love is kinder, more complicated and requires wanting the best for the other person even if what's best for them ends up not being you.

And I do love Jack.

I love the way he pays attention to the things I care about and actively listens. We have a similar sense of humor. We both love to read and can sit for hours, side by side, content to be together without having to say a word.

The sex is ah-maz-ing.

I can't imagine being happier.

Still, I'm determined to get real answers for Jack, even though it seems like every day that passes he's less concerned about what happened at the award dinner. I overheard part of a conversation between him and Hugh. It started with Jack saying he was ready to let that anger go.

Hugh responded that meant it was time to bring another man back and asked Jack if I knew anyone who might be willing.

Jack asked who Hugh was considering. Hugh mentioned a man named Edward who he considered the smartest man in the unit. I was tempted to jump to Jack's defense, but that comment didn't seem to bother Jack.

Jack doesn't measure himself by Hugh's opinion and I respect that. Hugh doesn't know that Jack came from an upper class background. He doesn't know that Jack had an Ivy League education or how well-read Jack is.

Hugh is a good man, but he takes things at face value. He's most comfortable when he has a plan and is following it. Jack lets Hugh lead, but it's clear Hugh's influence over him only extends so far.

It's also clear that Hugh has relied on Jack in the past to be the muscle behind every plan. Jack is taller, stronger, faster, and, in my opinion, smarter than Hugh—but he'd never say it.

Jack was raised humble and that is one of the many reasons I'd love him even if he was a man I met at work or at a café. I'm a nicer version of myself since he's come into my life and I never thought I'd say that about a man.

My interest was piqued when I heard Jack tell Hugh he was right about not bringing Ray back yet. He said there are still too many unknowns and Ray lacks the patience and self-control to hunt for answers in a way that wouldn't expose all of us to danger.

So Ray, according to Jack, should be the last one they

free. Knowing how Jack cares for Ray, and how much Jack hates being a spoon, that had to be a difficult decision to come to.

Hugh spoke about how careful they had to be when choosing which utensil to find a mate for. Some of the marks were similar enough to be confused.

Not Ray's, though. His was covered with marks from years of abuse.

My heart broke when Hugh said, "Just because I don't trust Ray, that doesn't mean I have no compassion for what made him the way he is. I cut off my own finger in an accident. You were born blind. When you told me Ray's father was the reason he was wheelchair bound before Project Inkwell, I understood his rage—but you were the only one who could convince him to contain it. Without you in the mix, I would have killed Ray or he would have killed me. And, honestly, I'm not sure he wasn't responsible for what happened to us."

"Don't say that, Hugh. He might know what happened, but we took an oath to protect each other."

Hugh didn't have an answer to that, and the whole conversation gave me chills so I walked away from it.

My phone rings in my pocket. It's Greg. I let it go to voicemail. I should talk to him. We're friends, but so much is already going on that it's easier to avoid him. I feel the same about Ashley.

What should I tell them?

How much is safe to say?

I want to spill everything, but my loyalty is with Jack, and as long as my silence doesn't endanger my friends I feel like I shouldn't say anything to them. Not yet. For the same reason Jack has yet to contact his family. We need to know that what we're doing won't put anyone else in danger.

My phone rings again. It's Ashley.

She's already texted me twice today. I can't let her think I'm upset with her. I'll tell her . . . something. I don't know what. I answer, "Hey, Ashley."

"You are in so much trouble," she says, but there's humor in her voice.

"I am?" I sit down on the arm of my couch. "What did I do?"

I bet she found out I quit my job.

"I went to see Mercedes this morning because . . . well, she answers texts. Anyway, I was thinking about how you said we were wrong about her and I offered her some muffins and some coffee as a little apology. And you're never going to believe what she showed me."

My mouth goes dry. "What?"

"Her silverware collection . . ."

Now I can't breathe. "Did she?"

"She did. And I thought she was crazy when she told me to run my hand over them and see if any of them called to me. I mean, it sounded insane. She's really persuasive, though, and you know I like to laugh so I did it. And you're not going to believe . . ."

I might pass out. "What won't I believe?"

"I left with *a knife.* Do you still have your spoon? I know I joked that you should play with it a little, but now I'm thinking there might be something to this. I can't begin to describe how fucking attached I feel to this knife. I'm back in my apartment and it's in my purse, but I keep thinking about it. When I held it . . . I wouldn't tell anyone else this . . . but you know when the hero in a romance says MINE and we melt? I swear on my life that I felt the knife say that to me. We need to talk. Is Mercedes some kind of witch? Hypnotist? Did I just join a cutlery cult?"

In a rush, I say, "Whatever you think you should or shouldn't do with that knife, Ashley, you shouldn't. You need to be really, really careful with it."

"No kidding, it's a dinner knife, but it's surprisingly sharp."

Trying not to panic, I ask, "This knife, is it covered with little marks?"

"It is."

Oh, God. Oh, God. "You need to give it back to Mercedes. Right now."

"I don't want to."

I remember feeling exactly the same. The bond was so intense. "Ashley, you need to trust me. *Do not* fuck that knife."

She laughs. "*Ouch* and of course I won't. What kind of

freak do you think I am?"

"Swear to me. *Swear*. Keep your clothes on. In fact, go for a walk outside until I get there. Do not be alone with that knife until after I explain to you why you need to give it back."

"Dramatic much? Sure. Okay. I'll take the knife for a walk."

"Leave it in your apartment, Ashley. Walk away from it—right now."

"Are you okay, Cheryl? I only called you because this shit is funny, but you're freaking me out."

I'm on my feet and frantically searching for my car keys. "I'll be there before you know it. Meet me at the sandwich shop next to your house. And don't bring the knife. Please."

"Okay, okay, whatever. I'll meet you at the sandwich shop near your house."

"I'm sorry I didn't tell you everything earlier. This is all my fault."

I find my keys, end the call, and as I'm rushing out the door, I call Jack. As soon as he answers, I blurt, "Mercedes gave Ray to Ashley."

"What?"

"My friend Ashley has Ray. He's still a knife, but she has feelings for him already . . . you know what kind of feelings I'm talking about."

"That's not good."

"I know." I'm hyperventilating a little as I start my car.

"I'm heading over there now."

"I'll come too. Hugh stepped into a store to grab a water. As soon as he's back we'll head to where you are."

"No. She doesn't know about you." I pull out of my spot and nearly back into a black SUV that looks like it's waiting for a parking spot even though several are available. The driver doesn't react with any of the road rage I would have expected, and that's a good thing because I have much more pressing things on my mind.

Will Ashley believe me if Jack isn't there?

I wouldn't have.

"Okay," I give Jack the address of the sandwich shop. "You should come, but Ashley doesn't know anything yet. This is going to be a shock for her."

"Why Ray? Why of all the silverware would Mercedes choose him?"

"She didn't choose him, Ashley did. Or Ray chose her. I don't know."

"It'll be okay, Cheryl. I'll make sure it is."

My breathing calms and I wipe a tear from the corner of my eye. I am afraid, but I'm not alone, and that makes all the difference.

"I love you, Jack."

"I love you too, Cheryl."

"I shouldn't have, but I overheard your conversation with Hugh about Ray. How dangerous is he?"

Jack is silent for a moment, long enough for me to realize

how serious this was. "I don't know, but I'll handle it."

"No," I say firmly. "We'll handle it. No one messes with *my* spoon."

"I do like it when you get possessive."

I flush and marvel how I can be both nervous and turned on at the same time. "I'm trying not to be. You could help a girl out by being a little less amazing."

"Hey, after we put out this fire, what do you say we get a gallon of ice cream and have a little fun."

I shoot through a yellow traffic light and notice the black SUV goes through the red almost as if it's trying to keep up with me. "Jack?"

"Yes?"

"I think I'm being followed."

"Don't go to meet Ashley. Keep driving in the city. Don't take any side roads. I need a car of my own. I have your location on my phone. We're coming to you."

"Okay."

After a moment, I say, "Jack?"

"Yes."

"Be careful."

The End for now . . .

For more about what happened at the award dinner and to meet another super soldier read Knifed: A Lighthearted Utensil Romance, book 3 (Ray)

Enjoy my sense of humor? I'm known for my sweet but spicy billionaire series. Start with *Maid for the Billionaire*; it has all the escapism romance and humor without the cutlery. It's binge reading at its best with more than 40 stand-alone books set in the same billionaire world.

About the Author

Ruth Cardello was born the youngest of 11 children in a small city in southern Massachusetts. She spent her young adult years moving as far away as she could from her large extended family. She lived in Boston, Paris, Orlando, New York—then came full circle and moved back to New England. She now happily lives one town over from the one she was born in. For her, family trumped the warmer weather and international scene.

She was an educator for 20 years, the last 11 as a kindergarten teacher. When her school district began cutting jobs, Ruth turned a serious eye toward her second love—writing and has never been happier. When she's not writing, you can find her chasing her children around her small farm, riding her horses, or connecting with her readers online.

Contact Ruth:

Website: RuthCardello.com
Email: RCardello@RuthCardello.com
FaceBook: Author Ruth Cardello
TikTok: tiktok.com/@author.ruthcardello

Made in the USA
Columbia, SC
22 December 2024

50229513R00096